Bundle at the Threshold

by

Rocco Russo, Jr.

PublishAmerica
Baltimore

First printing

All characters appearing in this work are fictitious. Any resemblance to real persons, living or dead, is purely coincidental.

ISBN: 1-4241-2942-7
PUBLISHED BY PUBLISHAMERICA, LLLP
www.publishamerica.com
Baltimore

Printed in the United States of America

In loving memory of

SASHA
DADDY'S PRINCESS

Forever in my heart

To my wife Linda, my dearest friend and loving companion. For being you, and for being there for the last thirty-six years of my life, I thank you from the bottom of my heart. Your support, devotion, and belief in me made it possible for me to reach my star. For what I am, I am because of you, and a man could never be more blessed than I.

Love has no end.

I would like to thank my friends and members of my family, especially Rocco III, Rocco IV, and Francesca Russo, whose love and support have inspired me immensely.

A special thanks to Marianna Heusler for all her advice, encouragement, and friendship.

Special thoughts for my good friend Vincent Barile whose courage and strength I admire and who taught me to always look at life's brighter side with a smile.

Chapter I

The Interview

Riding eastbound in heavy traffic on a suburban, London road, frustrated by the morning rush, the only sign of relief was the car radio which had just forecasted the day's weather, followed by a short announcement noting that at the sound of the tone it would be eight A.M.

Margaret McCall, who had not had a decent cup of coffee that morning or a bite to eat, was in a bit of a hurry for her scheduled appointment at the Carfax Nursing Home. So excited was she with her new assignment. A freelance reporter, she sold her stories to tabloids, magazines, and occasionally was lucky enough to land a short exclusive for a major newspaper.

A particular case in the archive files of unsolved crimes had caught her attention and, most of all, her curious interest. Both unique and bizarre, it had baffled the police for more than half a century, remaining unsolved. For within that time, in the year 1891, seven murders had been committed, and the law, labeling this case to be one of the most extraordinary since the infamous bloodbath of Jack the Ripper, had prosecuted not a single soul or suspect.

Scottish, born in a small town of Aberfeldy Tay, between the highlands and the grassy, rolling hills of Scotland, she moved to England in the heart of London just after receiving her degree in journalism. At the age of twenty-four, bright-eyed and highly intelligent, the fiery redhead had a taste for adventure and intrigue and an overwhelming love for freelancing, which allowed her to do her job at her own pace without the intervention of a boss.

Although usually calm and confident, today she felt pressured as well as nervous. For today was most important for Margaret who had gone through great lengths to arrange this appointment and meet face to face with the detective who had been on that case at that time. Although the year was 1955 and the inspector was now eighty-nine years of age, it was remarkable to learn from Doctor Lange that Inspector Thomas Gibbs' mind was as fresh as the day he had conducted his investigation some sixty-four years prior.

Making a sharp right off the main road, Margaret drove up the slight incline lined with cedar trees and pulled into the parking lot of the establishment, not having the slightest trouble finding a space. Taking the short walk upon the flagstone path, she entered the home, heading straight for the information desk. Inquiring about her meeting with Dr. Lange, she presented her identification, confirming her appointment with Inspector Gibbs. Told to take a seat, she sat across from the desk in the spacious lounge and picked up a magazine, thumbing through the pages to pass the time as she waited.

Some twenty-five minutes later, Doctor Lange made his appearance from out of the elevator, and after making a quick scan and not seeing anyone else waiting in the lounge, he assumed she was his appointment and walked directly to her.

With a quick handshake, greeting her with a warm smile, he sat next to her and expressed his apologies for having had her wait so long. Standing now, he asked Margaret to follow him as he walked to the elevator and pushed the button. While they waited, he explained that Inspector Gibbs would be most happy to see her since he very rarely had any visitors.

Walking through the corridor on the fourth floor, they passed the head desk and turned right, entering into the solarium, one of Inspector Gibbs' favorite resting places. As they stood by the door, Doctor Lange remarked how often Inspector Gibbs relived the past and had never forgotten the incident, repeating his story to anyone who would listen, making the residents so disgusted from hearing it time and again that they often avoided him. However, since her expected visit, his spirits had been lifted, pleased that he had finally found a person who would listen to him from start to finish.

Now pointing to the far corner of the plant-filled room lined with skylights and with rays of sun that warmed the bodies of the aging, Doctor Lange led the way to introduce Margaret to the inspector.

At first glance, he was not as she had expected. She somehow had visualized him to appear differently—tall, clean-shaven with hair neatly combed, and intellectual looking. But much to her surprise, he was quite the opposite. Fast asleep, cuddled in his chair, his arms were folded across his rather large potbelly and age spots covered his scalp and baldhead. It was also obvious that he wore the residue of his many meals. His tainted beard and food stained shirt undoubtedly were an eyesore for neatness and dispelled all her expectations.

As Dr. Lange tapped him gently on his shoulder, trying not to startle him from his pleasant nap, Gibbs woke to see the pretty face of a young woman looking down at him. He rubbed his eyes, smiled, and replied in a low voice, "I'm very pleased to meet you. You must be Margaret McCall."

With a handshake, now smiling as their eyes met, Margaret greeted Inspector Gibbs and asked, "How do you know that?"

Gibbs, a bit of a jokester, answered, "You must have forgotten. I was an inspector, remember?" Quickly adding, "Only kidding. I saw your picture in a magazine that I was reading, and I admit I was very impressed."

Excusing himself, Doctor Lange turned to Margaret, "Please forgive me. I must make my rounds. I am sure you and Inspector Gibbs have much to discuss, so I'll leave you two to continue your conversation."

Left alone, the two looked silently at each other for a short time until

Gibbs broke the mood by asking her where he should start. Not wanting to miss anything, Margaret quickly replied, "From the beginning, if you don't mind. I am very interested in hearing every detail."

Pulling up a chair, she sat across from him, taking out a pad and pencil from her attaché case, and looking straight at him, she commented, "I'm ready whenever you are, Mr. Gibbs."

Taking a deep breath, Gibbs expressed some concern. He wanted Margaret to understand that although many clues, events, and information had come to his knowledge at different times before piecing the puzzle together, he felt it best and easier for her if he explained the whole story in its chronological order.

Chapter II

The Abandonment

It was the day before All Hallows' Eve in 1876 when a prostitute named Nancy Wales gave birth to a baby boy during the night. Nancy, a young, impoverished woman of nineteen, at first glance seemed a bit younger than she was. Short, slim built, with brown eyes and shoulder length, brown hair, she was so uncontrollable and wild that she became a lady of the night.

On the other hand, her mother, whose name was Peggy, was altogether different. Well in her mid fifties, she walked with a slight limp and appeared untidy, not caring what others thought. Being a religious fanatic who filled her room like a shrine, she dedicated dozens of lit candles as offerings before her many saints.

Like any other mother, she wanted the best for her daughter, but she knew this was not possible and felt that Nancy's troubles were all due in part to her upbringing and the fact that she was fatherless.

On that rainy morning, a knock was heard at the door, and Peggy opened it to discover, there to her surprise, her daughter holding a baby. "Don't tell me this is your child?"

"Yes, it's your grandson. Doesn't he look pretty?"

11

"Good God, Nancy," shrieked Peggy. "What have you done? You know we don't have money for a baby. Why did you come here?"

"I had no place to go," she meekly replied. "Can I come in? I'm cold and tired and have to talk to you."

"I guess so. Do I have a choice? It seems you only come around when you are in trouble and need my help."

She knew her mother was right. She hadn't been to the house in a long time. Her mother looked older than she had remembered, tired and drawn. Walking into the living room, Nancy placed the baby on the armchair before the fireplace, and taking off her shawl, she asked, "All right if I sit in your chair and feed the baby? He hasn't eaten all morning."

"Yes, by all means, feed the poor child. He's probably starving. Have you given him a name?"

"No, not yet," she sighed. "I haven't given it much thought while I was recovering. He's only a few days old."

Still probing, Peggy continued, "Then where did you give birth?"

"In the Rocklin Inn."

"You mean in that rented room that your whore friends use as a pig sty?"

"Yeah, while to you they seem like the scum of the earth, to me they are my friends and gave me a place to give birth," Nancy defended.

"So why did you leave your whore friends?"

"Stop calling them that! Besides, it's not a place for a baby to stay, and I was told that the customers would be uncomfortable and not take kindly to a child. That's why I had to leave."

"Since you haven't mentioned it, I assume you don't know who the father is."

"What makes you think that?"

"Well, do you?" Peggy screamed.

"What's the sense of getting into it? You know I don't know," Nancy admitted. "So let's not talk of it anymore."

"So what are your plans? Did you think I would take care of him while you run around gallivanting?"

"Nah, not exactly. But I did hope you would watch him at times."

At that instant, Peggy blew into a rage. "If that's what you expect, you can leave now and take your child with you! I'm too old to raise a child. I don't see you for seven months. You don't stop by to see how I'm doing or if I'm still alive. You run around from man to man, giving little care for your life. Then you just pop in and say, 'Ma, can me and the baby stay with you?' I may love you, but I don't like you. And I don't like your whore friends and your whore ways. Do you hear me, Nancy? Your whore ways—filthy, disgusting, and sinful."

"Ma, your yelling is scaring my son and making him cry," Nancy interrupted. "Can you please stop? I'm really tired and weak and need to rest. Can't we argue over this another day when I feel stronger? Right now, I'll sleep on the floor next to the fireplace, if that's all right with you."

"No, that's no place for a baby. Take my room for now and I'll bed down someplace else," Peggy said, pulling her shawl tighter around her frail body.

As Nancy rose from the chair, Peggy, cooling down some, tossed a log onto the fire, and sitting in her chair, she observed a moment of silence. Staring off into the fire and with her weary mind filled with many thoughts, she reflected. She realized that Nancy's pattern was always the same, never seeing her daughter for months on end. But as a mother, how could she turn her away when she needed her the most? After all, Nancy was her only daughter, despite her many wrongs.

Peggy, depressed and troubled by the birth of this child, had barely enough food for herself, let alone an infant who required lots of milk and special food. Nevertheless, this was only minor, considering the real problem that upset Peggy. What really bothered her was that there was no ceremony before God and a consecration of marriage to follow, and as far as she was concerned, this was an act of blasphemy that had to be rectified.

It was a brisk night in November when Peggy made her decision. While Nancy slept, still trying to recover from her ordeal, Peggy quietly crept into the bedroom. She held her breath as she slipped the baby out from the covers. She prayed he would not cry and wake her daughter. Her hands trembled, but she knew this was the only solution.

13

Quickly, she made her way through the woods, firmly clutching the baby close to her chest, trying to shield him from the cold wind. She could see the house in the distance. She picked up her pace, wanting to get this over with before she changed her mind.

As she approached the house, having it all planned in advance, she quietly placed the wrapped baby on the doorstep of the residence, reasoning in her deranged mind that by doing this, she was putting evil where evil belonged. With a closed fist, she pounded on the door and dashed off, hiding behind a bush, watching with keen interest.

The owner of that residence was very wealthy. The entire estate had been left to her by her father, eight hundred seventy-seven acres of land along with a twenty-room mansion. For over a century, the family had inherited a reputation of witchery, and she was considered one as well by the town folk who cursed and damned her as an outcast with whom no one would dare associate. Attractive, short, and slim, she had long white hair that was most often kept in a French braid and accented by a black ribbon tied midway in a bow. Isabel Laughton, as she was called, was a recluse, and not having any other members in her household, she lived alone with the exception of a single servant, named Dutch.

On that fateful night, Isabel's dog was acting very peculiar, barking uncontrollably by the main entrance. Wanting to see what was disturbing him so much, she opened the door and was overtaken by shock. She could not believe her eyes as she saw a baby there; it was a dream all come true for her.

Getting down upon one knee, she gently picked up the child wrapped in a blanket as she felt a joyful rush flow through her body. Adoringly she cradled him in her arms, and that joyful feeling now became an instant bond of a mother's affection. At forty-six, she knew she was past her childbearing prime, although she yearned for one so badly. She had no intentions of saying a word to anyone, especially the authorities. After all, this was one opportunity that she was not going to let slip through her fingers; it was love at first sight and all she wanted to do was raise and care for him as her own.

At that moment, Dutch made his entry. Understandably a bit

surprised to see the child, Isabel took him into her confidence and asked that he be discreet and not mention a word to anyone of this night. Isabel did not worry too much about Dutch. After all, this powerful man of forty was unable to speak, mute since birth. Feared by most, he suffered from blindness of his right eye, which had badly discolored the pupil, turning it to pure white. Very tall, he was a little odd looking, probably due to his wild, white hair that was usually uncombed, his lack of expression, and his rigid, somewhat stiff, walk.

Despite his disablement, it did not impair his work. Living up to all her expectations and always having been loyal to her, she never expected him to fail her now.

******

The following morning, while Isabel was overjoyed with the prospect of motherhood, Peggy's mood was overshadowed by the grim despair of her actions.

That morning Nancy woke and turning to her side to glance at her son, she discovered him missing. She did not get excited nor think anything wrong; she just assumed that her mother had come to her senses and had taken the child to admire her grandson. But to Nancy's surprise, as she walked out of the bedroom and into the parlor, all she saw was her mother sitting in her chair, sipping a cup of tea, with her son nowhere to be found.

Excited, she screamed, "Where's my son?"

"He's in safe hands," Peggy quickly responded.

"What do you mean he's in safe hands?"

Jumping from her chair and turning sharply, Peggy snapped back, "I gave him to someone who is wealthy and can afford to take care of him—giving him a home and a life we can only dream of."

"Who gave you the right to give my son away? It's just like you to interfere and go behind my back without ever asking me what I feel or think about the idea."

"I know what's best, and I know you better than you know yourself. What I did was the right thing!"

"How can you say that? You don't know what I really feel."

"Who you fooling, Nancy? I know you're not the motherly type. There's no way you'd settle down and take care of this baby. Besides, this will give you a second chance to start your life over and meet a gentleman and, hopefully, marry respectfully."

"How do you know this family will love and care for him?"

"I believe she would. As I watched on, I saw her eyes light up the moment she discovered him. I could tell from her reaction that love was right from the start as she held him close to her heart. I'm more than sure there will be no problem and no need for you to worry."

"Do I know this woman?"

"For your own sake, I think it's best you don't know who she is." The last thing Peggy wanted her daughter to know was that she had entrusted her grandson to a witch.

Pausing for a moment, Nancy, still confused, reflected, "But, but I'm his mother and feel a little guilty about doing this."

"Oh, come on! Like I said, this would give you another opportunity, and I pray to God that you get over your whore ways and do the right thing this time."

"There you go again. Save your holier-than-thou attitude for someone else! I'm tired of you judging me and throwing it in my face." Wanting to hurt her mother, she lashed out, "You think you're so perfect, but you're really not much different than I am. Did you know my father's name?"

Head down, taking a deep breath, Peggy admitted, "No. I never did get to know his name."

"So why didn't you just leave me on a doorstep?" Nancy continued her tirade.

"There was a difference between us."

"What difference?"

"I wanted a child, but I know you don't really want your son. He'd be nothing but a burden for you. I admit I made mistakes in life, poor choices, but that doesn't mean you have to follow in my footsteps. You can make a better life this time. Perhaps, marry someone who has money. Being poor and not having a husband to help support the child could really make life stressful. Believe me, I lived through it. I know what I'm talking about. What I did, I did for your own good."

Giving it a moment of thought, Nancy was inclined to agree with her mother. She hated to admit it, but she really didn't have motherly instincts. She already felt overwhelmed, and she had only been a mother a few days. Taking a deep breath, and almost in a whisper, Nancy conceded, "Well, maybe you're right. Maybe I should just put the past behind me and start over again. It's probably for the best."

******

Isabel, on the other hand, now savored every moment of each day. Living with her newfound son was the answer to all her dreams; she had finally found peace in herself and the comfort of love. With the passing of a few years and their secret kept intact, she had never felt happier. Hidden within her shell, she broke the bonds of her imprisonment and rose to the climax of her love, one she never thought she was capable of achieving. Inspired by that one love she had not felt in such a long time, she had now found the true meaning of life and its purpose. Her aching heart that had been empty for so long was now fulfilled, and her spirits, which dwelled in the depths of her loneliness, now rose to the peak of contentment. Indeed, Isabel was a changed person.

Needing to be wanted and wanting to be needed, Shawn now became her inspiration, her life, her reason for living; for everything she did, she did for him. He was on her mind, in her heart, and in the depths of her soul. There was not a thing she would not do for him. Truly, she was his mother, and their love had grown strong in their relationship.

He was so innocent, and he made her feel that life was worth living. So many times when she was growing up she questioned her purpose in life but now she had no doubt. She could not have loved Shawn more if he were her own flesh and blood. She loved him unconditionally. When he looked at her and stretched out his little hand for her to take, she could barely hold back the tears of happiness. She was overprotective; she knew it, but he was like a highly prized treasure that she cherished and guarded.

As she watched him sleep, unaware of his past, poignant memories of her own past were sparked. Reminiscing those early years of her childhood, she thought back to those fond and wonderful days with her father. She noted there was never a more perfect relationship between father and daughter, and those unforgotten times had been the highlight of her life. Feeling a moment of despair, she could not help but feel the way she did. As the tears flowed down her cheeks, she realized well in her heart that those days were long past and could never be repeated.

She loved her father more than life itself. To her, he was all things; he was her love, her salvation, and most of all, he was her knight in shining armor. So proud she was of him that every time she saw him, her face lit with anticipation, bringing on a smile as he thoughtfully showered her with little gifts that were sealed with the affections of his hugs and kisses. He used to call her "my little angel" and she loved every minute of that, never forgetting that phrase, always considering herself as Papa's guardian angel.

For a second, a smile crossed her face, and she knew it was from the thoughts of her father that came to mind; the joys, the good times, the everlasting love that they shared for one another. That is perhaps why she had chosen that particular name for her son. It had a special meaning where she could honor and keep the memory of her father alive, and to her, there was no other name more appropriate than her father's name.

Unlike the bond she shared with her father, the mother-daughter relationship was somewhat of an unusual union. Their strained relationship seemed to be unsettled right from the start of Isabel's age of understanding. So much alike in character, they clashed constantly and were always at each other's throat. It was unnatural for them to act this way, but somehow through their stubbornness, neither one would submit to the other's supremacy.

Isabel's mother was very controlling; she had to have her way, so repetitious, verbally abusive, and so unbearable that you just gave in to shut her up. Short tempered, always thinking only of herself when she should have been thinking of her daughter, Isabel's mother was critical, uncaring, and never gave in, often hurtfully snapping at her that she could buy her own things when she grew up. Being compulsive, irrational, and temperamental were her strong personal traits; if ever a person could show more hostility toward another human being, it certainly was Isabel's mother. It would be a grave error to upset her, for when she angered, she would burst into an uncontrollable rage, getting so out of hand that she was capable of killing and not even know that she did it.

At a young age, Isabel tried hard to make her mother happy, but no matter how hard she tried, it always seemed like she did or said the wrong thing. She wanted her mother's love; all young children need a mother's love, but it just wasn't to be. As Isabel grew older, she stopped looking for her mother's acceptance and love for she had felt the wrath of her mother's anger, being a victim many times and reprimanded with the use of a switch.

Her father would intervene and use his own body to block the blows, feeling his wife exercised excessive force. This action of defense used to irritate Isabel's mother to no end and probably was the reason why she felt so jealous toward her daughter, for she knew her husband had lost his love for her and loved Isabel more, and that tormented her.

Not wanting to follow in her mother's footsteps, Isabel promised herself that she would always treat Shawn gently and make him know that he could talk to her freely and never be afraid to tell her anything. They spent many a night sitting on the porch, watching the lightning bugs and admiring the stars. He would clap his hands in delight as she sang little made up songs to him and told him stories. One extremely hot night when Shawn was about two years old, they were sitting on the swinging bench that Dutch had made when he stood up on it, put his arms around her neck, and gently kissed her on the cheek. It was one of her fondest memories.

Isabel brought her hand to her cheek and for a moment, it was as if her father was there with her again. She recalled how diplomatic her father tried to be, remaining neutral, not pressing the issue with his wife. The one thing he did not want to do was to upset her and to show his partiality for Isabel, knowing that his wife suffered from acute depression and was very suicidal. She could not remember the last time she and her husband were intimate. Avoiding her bedroom every night, she knew for certain he was indeed a changed man.

She accused her husband of infidelity, sneaking off into the bedchambers of the servants, rather than her own, and she vowed revenge one way or another. Coincidently, around the same time several deaths within the household were deemed strange as a few of the women servants died mysteriously and for no apparent reason. But Isabel's father knew better. His wife had had a hand in it, and although she denied it, claiming that their deaths were nothing more than accidents, he knew that she had poisoned them all.

But how could he turn his wife in; he was not the kind of person to harm anyone. After all, she was Isabel's mother, right or wrong, and he did not want to reflect himself as an uncaring person to his daughter. Despite his wife's many faults and their destroyed marriage, knowing that her family had a history of insanity, which would easily account for her rash behavior, he just left things as they were, totally disgusted with life. It was not long after her suicide that he passed on, and being discreet, he took with him the secret of his wife's madness to his grave.

Chapter III

The First Charm

By the time Shawn was a young lad of eight, he was considered an outcast by the locals which prevented him from having any other children his age with which to play. Isabel, who was saddened by the solitude that Shawn was suffering, did her very best to try and fill the gap by spending as much time as she could with him. But she knew in her heart he needed companionship, and most importantly, the friendship of another child with whom he could bond and share fun times.

She had felt the effects of a lonely childhood herself and knew what Shawn was going through. So to distract him from his loneliness, Isabel gave much of herself, creating adventures through long walks, storytelling, and mushroom hunting, which was one of her favorite pastimes. Yet it was not quite the same. Though Isabel did all she could to make Shawn happy, it was not enough in comparison to what a child his own age could offer. He needed that valuable contact, and this hurt and troubled Isabel to no end.

He was her whole world, and she his. Nurturing, supporting him every step of the way, she was the one he ran to when he was sad.

Although she felt like crying too whenever he was unhappy, she put up a front and hid her own tears, telling him that everything was going to be all right.

Having the advantage of riches, she was able to afford the best of schools, but school was not an option. So Isabel became his private tutor, teaching the curriculum well to give Shawn the finest of education. Nevertheless, this was in no way an escape from his misery. He still desperately needed the relationship of a friend, and Isabel, as well as Dutch, knew something had to be done soon.

Although Dutch felt a high regard for Shawn, he had never interfered with any of Isabel's decisions. Yet lately, for the first time in his life, he felt the need to act. Feeling the boy's pain, having been an outcast himself for most of his life, he knew the suffering Shawn was experiencing and could not stand to stay idly by any longer. Though he knew this was a delicate situation, he felt compelled to take the liberty of confronting Isabel over the matter. Having been employed by the family for such a long time, he felt he could relay his feelings without any fear of reprisal. After all, it was for her son's salvation. All these years, he had been privy to her most intimate secrets. She would understand that his involvement was prompted by genuine concerns for Shawn's well being.

Waiting for the best opportunity, Dutch approached Isabel as she watched Shawn play from the living room window. As Shawn sat alone upon a swing, beneath the massive branch of an oak tree, Dutch handed her his note and walked away, quickly returning to his many chores. She knew something was wrong. He usually wrote her little notes when he felt upset and wanted to express himself.

Opening the letter, she was amazed to find that his concerns were for Shawn as he conveyed his heartfelt feelings with deep emotion, "If you made it so, he could have a friend to play with."

Pausing, she reflected on his thoughts. She knew exactly to what he was referring. Even though she had been gifted with the powers of enchantment since childhood, she never felt the need to exercise such capabilities. Although she felt strongly against this decision, she debated over her options, torn between her heart and conscience. It had been so easy to make him happy when he was younger—a game, a new toy, but now that was not enough. As she again took another look at Shawn upon that swing, observing his loneliness, she ultimately put aside her qualms and gave in to her heart, knowing that Dutch's suggestion was justified.

The following day Shawn was in his usual place of play, occupying his time by the pond. Transfixed, observing the frogs swimming beneath the lily pads, he caught sight of the surface of the water, mirrored with a refection of a little girl walking toward him. Rising to his feet, he noticed a girl his age standing quietly by the edge of the pond.

At first reaction, he became captivated by her charm. He had no concept of where she had come from or who she was. With straight, brown hair that flowed down her back and big, brown eyes to match that were piercing and attractive, the rosy-cheeked girl, wearing a white dress, skipped over to him, introducing herself as Louise. As the rush of blood pumped with excitement in time to his heartbeat, he was overwhelmed by the joys of her presence, elated that he had finally found a friend to whom he could relate, especially one as feminine and as beautiful as Louise.

Once acquainted, he discovered she lived not far off from the forest and often played in this vicinity. Strangely, he had never seen her before. Their friendship blossomed quickly, and she promised that they would meet often. All he had to do was call out her name, and she would find him.

Explaining she had to leave, she turned away and as she left, he watched her cross the fields and enter into the woods where she soon vanished. At that precise moment, he felt he could fly and conquer the world. He had never felt this happy in his entire life. Ecstatic, he raced home, wanting to tell his mother of his newfound friend.

Over the days, Isabel saw a dramatic change over Shawn's life. He was no longer that solitary child stricken by loneliness, boredom, and depression. He instead became exhilarated, exuberant, wanting so much to continue his friendship with Louise.

Isabel was most happy for her son. She was sure Louise's

involvement would open the door to new avenues in his life, keeping him well occupied and content in the days to come, and this came as a relief to her.

Having now found his world expanded by his dear friend, they spent a great deal of time together, sharing good times of fun and laughter. Inspired by the love which she showed, Louise became his sentiment for life as he looked forward to his outings with her, promptly being there, never disappointing him. It was not as if her materialization was the result of a puff of smoke or a bright light that was blinding to the eye; she was there at the moment he began to speak. If he sat on his swing and spoke, she was behind him pushing him while she answered. If he was in the forest asking her a question, she was off to his shoulder picking flowers and responding. And if he lay down admiring the clouds and felt hungry, he would turn and she would be there by his side, offering him a bite of her apple.

Her comings were always obscure, never directly to his view. He felt it was a sort of game she was playing with him, but what did he care; just as long as they found one another, that was good enough for him.

Friends they remained, and each day Shawn found himself more and more enamored with Louise. As he grew older and matured, so did she, keeping the appearance of a young woman. She was his introduction to the best of nature's offerings and wonders. Her affection for the animals was her gift to him, passing on her interests and respect. Interacting beneath the forest canopy with their little furry friends, Shawn knew and loved all of the creatures, feeling the need to give each of them names. As they took their leisurely walks, seeking their animal friends as they paced along the way, they were bonded by tranquility and friendship. Together they made rustic birdhouses and planted species of plants that attracted birds and butterflies. The animals knew they meant them no harm, and animals that normally shied away from man were trusting of both Louise and Shawn. Although unable to converse with the animals because of their physical differences, they somehow understood him, which gave Shawn tremendous pleasure and satisfaction. For a lonely person who had never had a soul to associate with, he now had a girlfriend and a forest filled with friends, something he had never dreamed possible.

Motivated by their love for the animals, they took daily walks together, prompted to explore the forest life. Being very protective toward the animals, hunting and trapping were forbidden anywhere on the property. They made the woodland their domain and promised their animal friends a sanctuary free of harm under their watch.

Then one day, being at the right place at the right time, Shawn, now age fifteen, heard a rustling in the forest. Without hesitation, he intervened to prevent one of his friends from being shot. Having subdued a young, black bear that had retreated up a tree, a hunter was about ready to fire at the poor creature when Shawn, just in the nick of time, hit the gun up, making it discharge and miss his quarry.

At six feet, Shawn was already very large for his age and was equal to or stronger than the average man. With one hand, he pulled the gun from the hunter's grip and smashed the butt of it against the tree, destroying the weapon on contact. The hunter's shock quickly turned to anger. Furiously shouting profanities, he expressed his irritation and surprise at the drastic measures taken. Reluctant to fight someone twice his size or someone as determined as Shawn, he instead raised his fist and warned Shawn of the repercussions for this day.

With pride written on his face from a victory won, Shawn looked off into the background, delighted to see Louise smiling and applauding her victorious champion. It was like déjà vu, and he stood there remembering a dream he had recently had.

Turning to Louise, he felt the need to share it with her and question if she understood its meaning. "In the fallen snow, I saw a fox and was compelled to follow the creature. I did not know why I had to, but all I did know was that I was driven to do so by an unknown force. At first, I was able to keep pace with the fox, only being a step or two behind. Then the animal progressed in its stride, and the distance between us became much greater where I could barely make out the fox ahead of me in the haze of the snow. Shortly after, the fox was no longer visible, and all that I could see were its footprints, which I still curiously followed. My senses were now aroused, and I began to understand why the attraction of the chase gripped me. Apparently, the fox in his cleverness had been leading me to a scene where man's cruel domination over the animals was taking place. Observing the humiliation, I watched on as two men placed bets on a dogfight that was soon to proceed. You were off at a distance, and I could see that you were very distressed and tears were streaming down your face knowing that one of the dogs was to die needlessly in a vicious fight. I too felt this way, knowing that man's indiscretion would prompt such barbarism and seek pleasure and profit from an animal's death. I felt their wickedness and was overwhelmed. I could not allow this to happen and had to intervene and put a stop to this horrible action. I felt a mighty power over them, which I could not explain, and yet it was pleasurable. I had control, my commands were law, and they obeyed. Setting the dogs free, they ran off taking different paths. I wanted the men to feel what it was like to be pitted against one another in a situation where one of them was going to die. With that concept, they could feel the agony and pain of the tournament and experience death's threshold at a moment's notice. I was sure once they had, they would inevitably be reformed. However, I woke up before knowing the answer. Louise, what do you think the dream was telling me?"

Looking up, he was not surprised to see Louise's eyes welled with tears. She was so sensitive, her emotions so close to the surface. That's what he loved about her. Taking a moment to compose herself, she began, "I believe your dream was a premonition of a disaster that was to come. The fox represented your alertness, the unknown force was your instinct, and the footprints in the chase were a direction for you to take with persistence. All of those characteristics were signs of guidance foretold to you—the intervention by your actions, saving the bear cub, and dispensing justice. Waking up, not knowing the answer of whether the men had reformed, leaves man to his own questionable conscience, where the outcome remains to be seen."

Taking her hand in his, quietly they sat, not saying another word, just enjoying their time together.

Chapter IV

A Change of Heart

As Shawn approached manhood, Isabel had a change of heart toward the relationship her son shared with Louise. She felt that as he grew older, so would his needs as a man. She came to rationalize that he would eventually be hurt by the truth if he grew to love Louise more than just a friend, which she had witnessed was happening. Even though Isabel's creation personified an individual who was tangible and who could think and communicate, there was still one flaw; although they could be intimate, Louise could not bear children. That would mean that Isabel would never know the joys of being a grandmother, and loving children as much as she did, she would be deprived of this immense pleasure, something she really dreaded. Although their relationship was fine while they were children, it now posed many more problems as he matured.

She was aware that initially he would miss Louise very much and no doubt would suffer a broken heart. She also anticipated that this would eventually pass as time healed all wounds. After all, her son was tall, very good looking, and would become a man soon; he would meet other women in his life and eventually forget Louise.

Mulling it over and over in her mind before making the final decision, Isabel was filled with regret, knowing how the repercussions of her decisions would affect her son. Nevertheless, her instincts told her that the longer she waited, the harder the impact would be. She had to put an end to this relationship at once.

Little by little, Isabel made Louise meet Shawn less and less, hoping to minimize his dependence on her before arranging for Louise to deliver the dreadful news. Explaining to him that she had to go away and would not be seeing him ever again, he just stood there dumbfounded, trying to process the words he had just heard Louise utter. It was as if his world had just collapsed and had suddenly become so dark. He had never felt that this would ever happen, having believed that their friendship would outlast time.

For the first time in his life, he experienced both love and pain simultaneously, and he begged her to stay. But it was not to be, and losing Louise, he came face to face with his anguish, realizing his love for her was far more than just friendship. With tears streaming down his cheeks, he embraced her, holding her tightly, never wanting to let go. He was unable to control his emotions, and as he sobbed, Louise cried too. Breaking up inside, he stared adoringly at her, his eyes filled with regret, and Louise was able to feel him trembling.

Having no control over her own destiny, there was nothing she could do to change the outcome. Because of her love for him, she did not want to hurt him any more than necessary, and she tried her best to ease his pain. Not wanting to prolong his suffering, she broke their embrace and kissed him once. This was goodbye, and gently touching his face, their eyes locked one last time as she smiled, turned, and departed.

Helplessly standing there, he suddenly felt cold. Feeling all alone, his heart began to cry out as a part of him wanted to leave as well. While he watched her walk off in the distance, forever whispering her name, he was sure of two things—he would never forget her or this terrible day.

Chapter V

A Plea for Reconciliation

Around this same time, Peggy, the mother of the prostitute who had placed Shawn on Isabel's doorstep, felt remorse for her actions. Reliving her despicable deeds for the last fifteen years, she had plenty of time to contemplate her regrets. She had come to realize that Shawn was her flesh and blood, not only family but also her only grandchild, and as a woman, she had felt the repercussions of this for some time. Disturbed by her own behavior, she cursed the day she had done that awful act and felt she did not deserve to live. She contemplated suicide but being overly religious, decided against it, not wanting to add any other sins to her already blackened soul. Not finding relief from her tormented mind, she was indeed a haunted person. For even when she closed her eyes and tried to sleep, all she could see was her betrayal of that child as she walked away. So distraught by this, she even went so far as to cover her mirrors, not wanting to look upon her shameful face. This was something she had not told anyone. Keeping her secret bottled up for all those years, it had finally reached its peak, and she had become desperate and felt the need of spiritual help.

To ease her mind, she sought someone who would listen and give her guidance and absolution for her sins. Pressed by her distress, she finally decided to meet with the town's pastor and speak with the Reverend Edward Peterson, whom she could trust and to whom she could open her heart. Not wasting a moment of this precious night, she felt her soul was in peril, and being so concerned for her salvation, she left in haste.

Once entering the large gates of the church grounds, she walked past the graveyard, which led to the sacristy. Using her fist, she pounded hard against the door, waiting for a short time before a glow of a lantern reflected through the glass doors that soon opened. Met by a woman, Peggy expressed her urgency, elaborating that her calling was a matter of life and death and that it was imperative that she speak with Reverend Peterson at once. Seeing Peggy's anxiety, it was evident that she was a troubled woman. Inviting her to step into the lobby, she suggested that Peggy wait there while she informed the reverend of her presence. Sitting on the bench beside the door, she looked up at the ceiling and took a deep breath, when not long from out of the shadows, the reverend appeared.

Lighting several more candles to brighten up the dimly lit room, Reverend Peterson was well acquainted with Peggy, one of his most faithful parishioners. The tall, slim reverend with silver streaked hair and beard knew Peggy by name and inquired what was troubling her so much that she felt the need to call at that hour.

As soon as he looked at her eyes, he sensed her sadness. This caused her to burst into tears, crying uncontrollably. Gaining some control, she calmed down, wiping her tears with the handkerchief handed to her by the minister. Plagued by her guilty conscience, she renounced her wickedness by confiding, "I'm so ashamed. I deserve to die! I'm not worthy of God's grace and you'll probably look at me as a cruel and heartless person."

"Please Peggy, slow down! I don't understand what you are trying to tell me. Have you murdered someone?"

"No! Worse than that! I betrayed my own flesh and blood," she sobbed with quick breaths of grief.

"I'm still not following you. Try to explain in more detail. Calm down. I'm here to help. Remember God is very forgiving."

Head down, her eyes fixed on the pattern of the floor, she began, "Fifteen years ago, my daughter—you know my daughter, Nancy—appears at my door one night holding an infant—her child. You know the life she leads; I'm so ashamed of her. Where did I go wrong? Now she brings another life into the world. But her world is made up of prostitutes, strange men, and wild times. I ask you—Is that any way to raise a child? I know she was depending on me to help, but…but I barely had enough food or money for myself, let alone the needs of a child. I was desperate. I knew she didn't really want him. She was only nineteen and not the motherly type. So I crept into her bedroom as she was sleeping and took the child."

Stopping for a moment, she looked up at the reverend. His eyes showed his kind side and gave her the courage to continue, "I did it for her—for him—for us!" she stammered. "I tried not to look at his face as he lay wrapped in the blanket in my arms. I was afraid that if I did, I would change my mind. So I snuck out of the house and went to Isabel Laughton's home and placed him on her doorstep. I pounced hard on the door and ran and hid and watched on from a distance. Her dog started to bark, and I guess it scared the baby because he started to cry. Then Isabel, dressed in a robe, appeared at the door. She bent down on one knee, and she tenderly moved the blanket away from his face to get a better look at him. As she picked him up lovingly, she spoke to him, asking him how he got there. Her voice was sweet and gentle, not at all like I had imagined it to be. It was like she had been waiting for him her whole life. I watched her bring him inside and then left to face Nancy."

Intrigued by what he had just heard, the reverend questioned, "How did Nancy react? Did she go to Isabel to get him back?"

"At first she was angry, and we argued. But that's nothing new; it seems like every time we get together, we argue. But I think deep down she was relieved to be rid of him. I never told her about Isabel. I figured it was best not to tell her who had her son. Especially not Isabel—you know—being a witch and all."

"Well, I'm not entirely sure about that. I think the people in town have been less than kind to her. After all, she is God's child."

"More like the witch's child," Peggy jabbed. "Anyway, that night's been haunting me. I live with the memory often, and I regret my actions. Maybe I should have helped Nancy. Maybe he would have helped turn her life around. In any case, I did make a terrible mistake!" Pausing and feeling shaken, she nervously rubbed her hands together and continued, "You know, he is our flesh and blood, and I have this urgency to get him back, but I don't know how to go about it and thought you might help me."

"I can see your problem," Reverend Peterson said compassionately. "I'm not sure I have the answers. Fifteen years is a long time. I'm sure Isabel loves him dearly. Can you just walk into her life and take him away? Think of the boy! She's the only mother he knows."

"But she's not his mother! Not his blood! We are! Each day my daughter pressures me more and more to find out where he is. She wants him back. I want him back. I told her I would handle it. I don't want her getting involved. But I'm too afraid. Isabel is a very powerful force to reckon with."

"Be that as it may, this is a very delicate situation. Any mother who had raised a child for so long would be reluctant—no, let me rephrase that—definitely opposed to giving up her child. All I can recommend is that you talk to her and see what comes from it. I know you are a very religious person, Peggy. God will help you through this burdensome time and give you courage and guidance."

Peggy wasn't totally sure she had the courage to face Isabel, but she did feel better after pouring out her heart to the reverend. Although this was not a confession, before she left, she asked that the reverend keep their discussion confidential, and as a man of the cloth, he gave his word and agreed to do so.

Chapter VI

Life's Repercussions

Although Shawn was fifteen, it was the first time his overprotective mother allowed him to join Dutch on the ride into town to pick up supplies and provisions that were ordered in advance. He had never forgotten Louise, and she felt this would be a perfect diversion to take his mind off her. Shawn, who had never seen the town before, also felt that it would be good to visit Colchester while giving Dutch the helping hand he needed and enjoy the fellowship of his company.

Living on the outskirts of Colchester, the town was no more than a short, twenty-minute ride, and the lush, rolling hills of the countryside were a remarkable sight. Even though Colchester was no larger than a four-block radius, it was well developed for its time, having all the accommodations that a community would need, and was the only place a person could shop for miles around.

Situated in a valley, north of the Stour River and south of Chelmsford, Colchester was rather small in comparison to other major cities such as London and Liverpool. Surprisingly, it had its share of important establishments, family businesses specializing in livestock, butchering, and blacksmithing, even a general store. South of this district was the vicinity where the variety stores were located, while at the end of town were gatherings of little storefronts that weaved fine quality linen and cloth, as well as accommodating special orders for decorative draperies.

Just across from the material shops was the boot maker. Not only did he make boots designed for the active man, he was also capable, with a quick glance of his foot gauge, of making a variety of customized shoes to fit children as well as women. Though the boot and shoe store was owned by Neilson and son, his wife ran the seamstress business which she operated right next door. As a team, they were very enterprising. With her talents and skills as a dress and hat maker, she was most profitable, and by displaying her many fashions in her window along with good business policies, she attracted the interest of many a wandering eye.

Since the female consumers were abounding in this sector, there was one storekeeper who felt his goods should not be overlooked. Tempting the inner cravings of a woman's discerning taste were the rich smells and yummy sights of the baker's shop. Conveniently located right smack in the middle of this garment center was Jonathan's Bakery whose tasty cookies, lush cakes, and plump juicy muffins were the pleasure and delight of any sweet tooth.

All other businesses were located on the main road, which appropriately was called Main Street, while the town ordinances designated the side streets strictly for dwellings. Rows of single-family homes lined the streets with picket fences marking their borders, and across from the end of them was an open field used primarily for the commercial sector with slaughterhouses, stables, and barns.

Approaching north into town, you passed the local authorities, where the courthouse and law enforcers imposed order, and ironically, just past that was the town's tavern.

The town's tavern, the Rocklin Inn, was the daily stop on the coach route for the Hutchinson Transportation Company. Having an array of accommodations to suit the traveler as well as the town's customers with room, board, and refreshments, it was the place for escape of one's boredom on a night out of fun and relaxation. For the social gatherer, choices were many. Besides its wide assortment of many spirits, there was also the atmosphere of games and the pleasure of darts and chess to intrigue the hearty challenger and sharpen the intellectual mind. Olin Phibes, proprietor of this establishment, ran a tidy inn, keeping strict house rules and enforcing them vigorously, if necessary, discharging all those who failed to comply.

With conversation making their ride much quicker, Dutch made his first of three stops, parking his wagon in front of the general store. Dutch busily checked and confirmed the large order while Shawn carried out the crates through the front door and loaded the supplies onto the wagon.

On his fourth trip while carrying out a small barrel, three boys, itching to pick a fight, approached him. Shawn, quiet and very reserved, went about his chores, paying little attention to the boy who peeked over the side of the open wagon. While the other boys watched on with sinister grins across their faces, the boy nearest Shawn picked up a corn broom from out of the wagon and taunted him saying, "Is this the broom your mother uses to fly on?"

Shawn, mindful of the boy's intention, was in no mood for a fight, and not saying a word, he continued retrieving the rest of the order, ignoring the insult. Agitated from not getting a response, the boy repeated his remarks but this time used the tip of the broom to poke Shawn's back, provoking him once again by adding, "Did you not hear me? I was speaking to you."

He could not help himself. At that instant, he felt the rush of blood flow up to his face. Not able to take another moment of this abuse, he turned sharply and lunged at the boy unexpectedly, taking him down to the ground. As the fight accelerated, the other two boys joined in on their friend's behalf, giving Shawn a bit of a thrashing. It was then that Dutch exited the store, carrying a large barrel on his back.

Surprised by the skirmish, he reacted instantly, tossing the barrel onto the wagon and separating two of the boys, holding each of them at bay with his powerful arms. Now reduced to a one on one confrontation, Shawn began to get the better of the troublemaker. Beating the boy to a bloody pulp, knocking out two of his teeth, and giving him a swollen eye, this day of anguish and regret would be well remembered. Not wanting to endure any more pain, the boy threw up his arms and forfeited the fight as he retreated. Dutch, letting go of the other two boys, allowed them to run off as well, smiling to himself as they high-tailed away.

But things weren't as simple as they appeared. Little did he know that the uncle of the boy who had been beaten was the magistrate and that posed a serious problem for Shawn.

The parents of the boy who suffered the beating were outraged. Demanding justice, despite their son's guilt, they filed a complaint against Shawn for assault, even though the general store owner who had witnessed the whole affair confirmed the story to the police that Shawn was not at all the one who provoked the fight. After intense questioning, one of the boys involved in the fight admitted the truth, verifying Shawn's innocence. However, little did this testimony benefit Shawn or have any impact on his case since the magistrate, a family member, presided over the proceedings, suppressed evidence, manipulated the facts, and put out a warrant for Shawn's arrest.

The following day three constables accompanying the paddy wagon arrived before the main entrance of Shawn's home. Dutch, who answered the doorbell, was a bit shocked to see the police standing just outside. As the sergeant handed Dutch the warrant for Shawn's arrest, Shawn happened to be coming down the staircase to see who was at the door.

Spotting him from the open doorway, the police, without warning, rushed forward to apprehend him. Scared, he resisted their advances, which provoked them even more, and soon they were engaged in a bitter struggle. Dutch, seeing Shawn in trouble, naturally came to his defense, which intensified the skirmish, causing a loud ruckus and arousing Isabel's attention. Hearing shouts and the breaking of glass, she realized that something was terribly wrong. She raced down the stairs, only to be confronted by the police who already had been separated and kept at bay by Dutch. He would not allow them to harm Shawn. His size and expression substantiated his sincere opposition.

As the situation cooled down some, Isabel, still very upset, questioned the meaning of this intrusion, discovering that they had come to arrest Shawn for assault and place him in the town jail until a date could be set for his case to be heard. Isabel, not wanting to make the situation any worse than it already was, approached Shawn, gently touching his face, and promised that her lawyer would get to the bottom of this awful ordeal come first morning.

Now turning to Dutch, Isabel politely asked him to move aside and allow them to take Shawn into custody. Dutch's somber expression communicated his feelings that he was most reluctant to do so, and he had to be told twice by Isabel before he did comply, still watching tensely as they approached.

Forcefully taken, Shawn was locked in the jail coach, hauled away like some common criminal, and placed in a cell beneath the courthouse where he was to await his arraignment. For a boy of fifteen, this was an awful experience, and he felt violated, persecuted, and wrongly accused.

Locked in confinement, he was surrounded by dampness. Drops of moisture dripped off the walls and accumulated in puddles beneath his feet. Very uncomfortable in this solitary confinement, Shawn looked for the jailer but was unable to see his surroundings too well under the dimly lit lighting of a single lantern. Shouting, he tried to arouse someone to log his complaints. The disgusting stench of urine was so offensive to his senses; sickened to his stomach, he could hardly bear it. He thought to himself how awful these conditions were. He was not used to this sort of treatment that demeaned a human being to the pits of the gutter. Having no choice, he soon realized there was not a thing he could do to change his conditions. All he could do in the meantime was to sit back on the straw mattress and hope a reprieve would come very soon.

The following day Isabel and her lawyer were there at the courthouse as she had promised. While the lawyer spoke with the magistrate, Isabel was escorted below by a jailer to meet with her son. She was upset when she found him huddled in the corner of the room, resting his arms and head upon his knees, looking very depressed. Shawn, once seeing his mother, jumped up and ran over to the bars to greet her, and showering him with kisses and overwhelmed with pity, she began to cry. She was disturbed by the conditions of filth that her son had to endure, and her expression registered that feeling of discontent.

Not able to see her son as well as she had wanted, Isabel asked for more light but was rudely refused by the jailer. A craze suddenly came over her. She turned sharply toward him, and if it had not been for fear of reprisal against her son, she would have physically gouged out his eyes with her fingernails for denying her request. Controlling her frustrations, she asked once again, but this time her tone became firm and alarming. Calling the jailer a pig, she promised that he would soon look like one if he did not hastily comply with her wishes. The jailer, afraid of Isabel, was aware of her reputation as a witch and felt the probability of her carrying out her threats was very likely. Not wanting to anger her any more than she already was, he picked up the oil lantern, walked over to her, and held it while she conversed with her son.

By this time, the lawyer made his entry, and with a smile across his face, he announced he had good news. Convincing the magistrate of the youth's age, he was able to get a grant for Shawn to be released on his own recognizance and to reappear at a later date for his arraignment. With a click of the deadbolt unlocked, the jailer opened the cell door, and Shawn was free to leave.

Getting a reprieve, he felt reborn. Quickly hugging his mother, he wanted to leave this dreadful place and put behind him the horror he had suffered.

Waiting outside, minding the coach, was Dutch. Very pleased to see Shawn, he gave him a bear hug and a big smile. Anxious to leave Colchester, it was not long before they reached the mansion steps of the estate. As he exited the coach, Shawn felt a great relief come over him as he passed across the threshold of his home. Harbored by his mother's love, he felt the sanctuary of safety within these walls. Though he was stricken with hunger pains, not having eaten a single thing or able to sleep a wink while confined, exhaustion won over his hunger, and climbing the steps to his bedroom, he attended to his much-needed rest.

Chapter VII

A Mother's Scorn

While Shawn slept, Isabel, noticeably distressed, walked into the parlor where Dutch handed her a glass of sherry and tossed a few logs onto the gratings. He knew that when she was in this kind of mood, she liked the warming comfort of a burning fire. With a glance, he was aware that she wanted to be left alone, having much to consider, her mind indeed heavy.

Holding her glass of wine, she stood before the fireplace, staring in a trance, watching the flames dance before her face. She could feel her blood burning just as hot as the fire she was watching. The more she thought, the angrier she became. She was disturbed by how her son was falsely accused, hauled away like some wild beast, and thrown into that filthy cell. She was out for blood, and she wanted revenge. She craved punishment for all those responsible for her son's pain, and they would experience the wrath of a mother's anger.

She never had the need nor felt this way before. She had always had reservations against using her powers, but as a mother, her perception had now changed, and she felt compelled to come to her son's defense. She admitted she was always overprotective, but her love for him was so great, she could not control herself.

Restless, she exited the parlor and took the stairs, heading straight for a particular room in the attic. Here high up, she could look out her dormer terrace and view the fields of the countryside for over a mile. She had used this room many times before as a child, and it became one of her favorite spots when she felt like this. Here, with its peace and quiet, she could collect her thoughts undisturbed. Sitting by the terrace doors, she was puzzled, trying to figure out how to dispense punishment. She already considered the magistrate and felt it would be rightful and deserving to include the three boys as well. Yet the question of how kept hounding her.

Frustrated, she sat back in her armchair, looking up at the ceiling where she soon saw the solution to her problem. There between the board slats was a bat at rest, waiting for night to call. She was tickled to death at the thought of it. Nothing disastrous to point blame and nothing gruesome to draw suspicion, just an act of nature. Rabies. Yes, it was all so perfect, she contended.

It was not until the second day of Shawn's release that Isabel decided to initiate her first spell. That evening she sat in her armchair in the attic and waited patiently for dusk to make its approach. With the first signs of nightfall, she opened wide her terrace doors, giving her little creature the access of an easy flight. Since all four victims lived just minutes from one another, she planned to dispense with them all at the same time, sending her messenger of death.

She knew a bite from a bat was superficial. The bat was so light that while a person slept soundly, he would not feel a thing. Leaving less than a tenth of a drop of blood, it would go undetected and hardly be noticed. Easily mistaken as an insect bite, the victims would remain unaware of the potential danger that had just plagued them. But then it would all be too late. Once bitten, it would take three to twenty days before the disease would show signs of its effects. With the early signs of a virus, the boys would suffer watery eyes, vomiting, and nasal discharges, which would soon develop into painful spasms of the jaw. During the second phase of this incurable disease, they would experience dread aroused by the sounds of water. Swallowing would now become impossible, with profuse spitting and sneezing, which would become so unbearable that they might want to bite anyone close to them. Soon the symptoms would enter into their final stages, leading to a dramatic end. Finally, it would intensify until paralysis or exhaustion gave way to heart failure, or where in the midst of a convulsion, death would occur, eleven days after the initial sign.

With her charm, Isabel placed herself into a deep trance. Unifying the possession of embodiment with the creature, she was able to witness all through the eyes of the bat. With flight, she approached the first house, seeing that the boys slept with their windows wide open. Landing on the windowsill, she was happy to see that both brothers were sound asleep, each one cuddled in his single bed. So quiet and gentle was her approach that they had no idea of her presence, nor did they even feel the penetration of her bite. The room dark and obscure, it was a perfect setting. Blending into the cover of night undetected, she administered death in a moment's instance. Her task completed, she was satisfied, and she silently left the residence to seek out her next victim, so far having achieved three of her intended targets.

But the evening was not won; when it came to the magistrate, she was gravely disappointed. Having luck on his side, he slept with his windows closed, preventing the fiendish creature from inflicting its deadly virus.

In her armchair, still sitting in front of her terrace doors, Isabel was awakened this morning by the brightness of the sun. Displeased by the events of the night, she took to her feet and walked out onto the terrace, stopping before its perimeter wall. Although she was dismayed by the thought of her defeat, which did not yield to her desires, she was strengthened by the will and determination to accomplish her goal. She felt the magistrate had gotten off too easy and had deprived her of the satisfaction of revenge. After all, he was her main objective, and she was not going to let him off the hook any time soon.

As she gazed out upon the open field, she took note of a massive oak tree with five ravens all clustered on a large branch. As she watched, her attentions were drawn to the disturbance of the birds constantly crowing, and suddenly she was stricken with the revelation of multiple thoughts. Giving it serious consideration, she felt that this approach would pose no obstacles to prevent her from achieving her goal as last night had.

The magistrate would be out in the open during the day where he would be most vulnerable. It was a foolproof plan. It could not fail. He would be caught off guard. She knew that each morning he took the road adjacent to the cliffs on his way to the courthouse; this she already knew from last night's flight. It was on this route, she reasoned, where her best chance of succeeding and putting her plan into motion would be. She was sure this time there would be no escape for him.

Ending her depression over last night's failure, she smiled cleverly, feeling good about herself. Come tomorrow, she had a special surprise in store for the magistrate, and she was sure he would pay the ultimate price—his life.

******

Early the next morning, the magistrate woke to a brilliant sunrise; opening his window and shutter, he greeted the day by stretching as he breathed in the fresh air. After washing himself at his dry sink, he donned his usual clothes and sat at the head of the table as he had done every morning for the past fourteen years of his marriage. His wife, who was already up and busily cooking his breakfast, prepared his favorite foods of flat cakes, a cup of tea, and one egg, soft boiled with two strips of bacon. Although this was pretty hardy for a person of his size and weight, the magistrate, a man in his mid sixties, was quite slim, actually underweight, and not at all tall. In fact, he was rather short, five feet five inches to be precise. Yet sitting in his courthouse, presiding high on his bench, as he looked down upon the accused, he had the appearance of a very tall person.

Kissing his wife goodbye, he saddled Bess, his horse, and rode to the courthouse as he did every morning. Just a short fifteen minutes from the outskirts of town, he was expected today to conduct hearings on two drunken disorderly cases.

Without warning, as he approached the vicinity of the cliffs, something dark struck his right eye, instantly causing tremendous pain. Falling from his horse, he struggled to raise himself to his knees as a shadow of that same figure reappeared suddenly, striking this time the corner of his left eye. The blows were sharp and firm; he was unable to see his assailant and could not understand what exactly was happening to him. With water-filled eyes, mixed with a bit of blood, his vision was obscured, and he was unable to see where he was. While trying desperately to locate his horse, a second barrage of blows struck simultaneously, and losing what little light he once had, all became total darkness.

Rolling on the ground from the excruciating pain he suffered, he felt his wounds, horrified as he realized that his eyeballs had been gouged out of their sockets. The thought of it sickened him to the pit of his stomach, and in a panic, he shouted for someone to help him.

Blinded, there was not very much he could do. Each time he tried to raise himself to his feet, he fell just as quickly. He felt his only chance for survival was to find his horse. Bess had made this trip so often that she knew the trail by heart and would take him safely back to town. Forced by necessity, he again tried to struggle to his feet. Calling for Bess, he thought he heard her in the direction ahead of him and followed that sound, walking with both arms extended before him, guiding his way. But unbeknownst to him, it was the flapping of the ravens' wings who were perched on a branch that had aroused his attention. Continuing toward the cliff's edge, he fell, hitting the rocks thirty feet below.

Around noon, the magistrate's horse came walking into town all alone and stopped before the courthouse where she usually rested. The court clerk, who had been sitting outside waiting for the judge, became a little concerned since he was missing and three hours late. Finding the situation a bit peculiar, they reasoned his absence was due to an accident and perhaps he needed help, so they gathered a search party to scour the countryside. Despite backtracking his path from town, right up to the doorstep of his home, not the slightest clue could be found for his disappearance.

******

The following day Isabel returned to her attic carrying a large bowl filled with cracked corn. As she opened her terrace doors, she beheld the five birds all perched on her balcony rail waiting for her to appear. She was delighted and gratified by her pets' performance, and she wanted to give them all a reward for a job well done. Justice had been served, and now that the magistrate had met his demise, she could not have felt any happier. Placing the bowl down for her pets, she stroked each one gently across its crown with her finger. A smile emanating from her sure pleasure, she took a deep breath, relieved to know that the punishment had gone better than anticipated.

It was not until the third day that the body of the magistrate was discovered. A group of men, who had been out early in the morning, hunting quail among the rocks of the cliff stumbled across his body. Transferred to the town's mortuary, there he remained undisturbed and preserved as evidence for the process of an impending autopsy and police examination.

The death of the magistrate was a great shock to everyone in the town of Colchester. Never in its time was there such a high-profile case as this, and it became the prime topic of conversation. Being a quiet and peaceful town where nothing really happened, the strange death stirred up much controversy among the people who did plenty of finger pointing, casting suspicion, and attributing blame.

Well aware of Shawn's recent arrest brought speculation by some that Isabel was so angered by her son's treatment that she cast a spell on the magistrate, causing his death. While others, with their wild accusations and their imaginations out of control, felt it was nothing more than outright murder where Shawn had killed him out of retribution.

Whatever the belief might have been, another incident added strong implications toward their way of thinking and that was the three boys who all suddenly contracted rabies. Deemed most strange, it was common thinking that they had all been bewitched.

Already manifesting symptoms of the disease, the town doctor diagnosed that all three boys were stricken and had to be placed in quarantine for at least a month. For the safety of their families and others, this measure had to be strictly enforced and made certain that there would be no contact whatsoever with anyone. The community leader, not prepared for this, was faced with the newly created problem of not having a place to house the boys to keep the spread of the disease under control.

At first thought, the jail was considered a suitable place to harbor the boys. Having four cells, they could occupy three of the four with the remaining one used for the town's arrest. Yet there were those who opposed this, feeling it would create a serious problem. The feces and urine would cause a health risk to all, not only to the caretakers who were deathly afraid of contracting the deadly disease but to any other prisoner confined in the fourth cell. There was also the worry of disinfecting the cells. After all, they could not be absolutely sure that the infectious germs were completely killed. Finally, after a heated debate and the argument growing more intense, one member came up with a brilliant solution.

Suggesting the old mill since it was abandoned and run down, why not use it to house the boys? It would serve the purpose; the boys could be shackled to the millstone, fed daily, and if the disease did happen to turn full-blown as predicted, there would be no worry of spreading the virus any further. Once the boys died, all that would be left to do would be to burn the place down, killing off all traces of the disease.

It was too much of a coincidence, the locals thought. It did not happen to just one or two, but strangely enough to all three and the same three who were involved in the fight with Shawn. It had to be the evil eye, they contended.

However, it was 1891, and this sort of thing did not exist anymore in these modern times. Black magic and witchery were a thing of the past, and the persecution of witches was banished well over one hundred twenty years ago. Yet those were the views of a handful that felt differently and insisted that extraordinary accusations required extraordinary proof. Nevertheless, this was an old town, and most of their thinking was still the old way. Unswayed, they had their own suspicions and beliefs, and you could not convince them otherwise.

Chapter VIII

The Intervention of Scotland Yard

Because the death was of a high official of the court, this constituted investigation by Scotland Yard. Dispatched from London immediately to oversee this case was Inspector Thomas Gibbs of homicide, along with his assistant Sergeant Peter Moore. With a projected day's ride along the countryside on rail and the rest of the way by coach, they were expected to arrive in Colchester late that evening.

With the arrival of the Hutchinson Transportation Company pulling into its final stop before the Rocklin Inn, the inspector along with his assistant, tired from their long day's journey, disembarked and acquired rooms for their stay. Aware of the complexities of this investigation, they would be there for the duration of the case.

Having much to do the following day, Inspector Gibbs retired early to his bedside, knowing he had to be at the mortuary come first morning to examine the body. With only five hours of sleep, normally an early riser and not requiring much rest, he was up at the crack of dawn, washed, and already dressed. Exiting his quarters, he crossed the hall to the opposite room, and knocking hard upon the door, he announced to the sergeant that he would meet him downstairs for breakfast.

Together they enjoyed a delightful meal of eggs and muffins, along with their usual cups of black tea. The two detectives, after acquiring directions, wasted not a moment as they headed to the mortuary. Though expected to meet this morning with Doctor Lane, who was head of the department, Gibbs was there to make his own inspection as well, and the doctor, who had already completed his pre-examination, waited for the inspector to perform his before beginning the autopsy.

Pulling down the white sheet that covered the body, Inspector Gibbs paused for a second. Feeling a chill at the gruesome sight of the magistrate's eyes, it was evident that some pointy object had repeatedly been used to poke them out. From what he observed, he did not believe that a knife had made these wounds. Definitely ruling out an accident, he firmly believed foul play was at hand, and this was indeed murder.

It was the bleeding of the eyes, which made him suspicious. It was obvious that death had occurred after the wounds were inflicted. He concluded that at the moment of the fall, which terminated the magistrate's life, death would have stopped his heart from pumping. In which case, if the eyes were removed after he fell, there would have been no bleeding, indicating to him that the inflictions had to occur before the fall. This much was clear, and Doctor Lane felt the same, ruling out an accident and verifying murder.

Now thoughts began to flow and many questions arose. Why? How? Who? When it came to his first question of why, he theorized that it could have been an act of torture; perhaps the killer wanted him to suffer before he threw him off the cliff. As for how it was done, he was not at all sure, but according to the wounds, he was positive that the weapon used was not a knife. A knife would have made jabbing slit marks upon the eyes and scalp, and this was not at all the case. He felt it must have been something round and pointy, like a sharp stick or a branch whittled to a point. Now he was left with the toughest scenario and that was who. Not having interviewed a single person at this point, it was hard to say. In the first place, he had to know who had a motive. Aware that the motive could have included a number of factors such as revenge, hatred, jealousy, or even possibly a ritual, without further investigation of the situation, he was unable to draw any more conclusions. He had to conduct more research, see the crime scene for himself, examine where the death took place, and perhaps from there he could discover additional clues to the puzzle.

The day still young, an open coach was arranged with the town's police to escort Inspectors Gibbs and Moore to the site where the crime was believed to have taken place. The town's constable had not made an official inquiry into this investigation. Except for the removal of the body found at the bottom of the cliff, whatever evidence that might still be around was preserved for Scotland Yard to investigate.

At the first inspection of the road, Inspector Gibbs could not find anything significant, just common traffic prints traveling to and from town and several black feathers along the roadside.

Gibbs asked the constable where the magistrate had fallen and if anyone had walked about the area and was relieved to hear that the crime scene had remained untouched. Pointing to a tree at the edge of a cliff, the constable made note of the spot believed to be where the magistrate had died.

While the constable and Inspector Moore stood behind and watched, Inspector Gibbs approached the cliff alone. He did not want to disturb or add any other footprints that might be misread. Taking his time, he examined every inch before taking his next step, cautious not to destroy any evidence.

As he approached the cliff's edge, he noticed in the soft sand a single set of prints of normal stride showing they had walked right off the cliff. Dumbfounded, he looked around and around for another set of prints, but none was to be detected. This was most extraordinary, he thought to himself. He could not, for the life of him, understand the reason why someone would do this. There were no signs of a second person involved, no push, no struggle, not even an indication that he was led, just a single set of prints, willfully walking off. For the moment, suicide came to mind. But this was not practical; why would someone pluck out his eyes just to walk off a cliff and kill himself? The whole scenario did not make a bit of sense, except to add more complications to an already confusing case.

Puzzled, he walked back to the carriage where he confronted the constable, asking him how far the magistrate's house was. Learning it was only a ten-minute ride, he decided to pay a visit to the house and speak to the wife.

On arrival, she appeared humble and weak, and the inspector could see she was in a state of depression, still mourning the loss of her husband. He did not intend to trouble her any more than needed, for now only asking permission to see the horse and saddle in the stable. Walking alongside of the horse, he stroked the animal's ribs and gently patted its rear as he passed from behind, stopping in front of the saddle. Strung over the stall where the saddle had been placed, he observed several drops of blood on its leather.

Finding these stains of blood now proved, without a doubt, his theory that the magistrate's inflictions had happened while he was on horseback, confirming his suspicions that death had occurred after he had been wounded. Not much to really go on. The criminal picture looked somewhat grim and bizarre, not making the least bit of sense. As it was, the inspector was left with a scene of an attack that started on horseback and accelerated, where the eyes of the deceased were poked out by some pointed object, blinding the magistrate. He was either led by someone or just happened to be walking in the wrong direction, not realizing the potential danger. But what really baffled him was why he couldn't find that second set of prints showing the attacker; it was as if the assailant vanished in thin air, not leaving a single trace.

Calling it a day late that afternoon, they decided to return to town, planning to have dinner that evening at the inn and enjoy a few drinks while relaxing. As they arrived for dinner, Gibbs noted that the house was filled with customers, some already feeling the effects of their drinks. Off to the far end were the loud debates of hot heads making their points, and to amuse the restless crowd was an attractive young woman entertainer, singing songs as she walked the floor. With a bar to the left and barrels stacked on the right, the center of the inn was set with tables for the dining area. Just across from there was a group who commonly used this corner for the pleasure of sports, indulging themselves in games such as chess and darts.

Luckily, a table had been reserved for the inspectors; this was due to the thoughtfulness of the innkeeper who now directed them to a table by the fireplace. Being a brisk evening, the comfort of the fireplace was a warm welcome, as well as providing a pleasant sight, for the two inspectors who were looking for an enjoyable night. Moments after they were seated, a waitress appeared carrying two mugs of ale and placed the goblets before them. She remarked that these drinks were compliments of the house, customarily given to all first time customers who dined there, and as soon as she took their orders, she dashed off to wait on other tables.

Enjoying their drinks while passing the time, the two inspectors engaged in friendly conversation, amused by some of the characters within the crowd. Not long after, a skirmish broke out. It seemed a man admiring the young, attractive entertainer got a bit carried away and had to be restrained. By then the waitress returned with their dinners and refilled their goblets to the rims. Smiling, she pleasantly remarked for them to enjoy their dinners and once again dashed off.

The smell of the pot roast was mouth watering, and not having had any lunch, occupied with their investigation all afternoon, they were quite hungry and eagerly delved into their food. Halfway through the meal, two men approached their table, quite drunk and a bit forward. Introducing himself as Eddie, he inquired whether they were from Scotland Yard and covering the magistrate's murder case. Gibbs replied that they were but were unable to speak of or make public their findings until the investigation was complete. Taking liberties, Eddie leaned on their table, and becoming a nuisance, he looked Gibbs straight in the face and commented, "I know you haven't found the killer yet, and if you'll be a good chap and buy me a drink, I will tell you who did it."

The innkeeper, seeing the men disturbing the inspectors, came over at once with the intentions of discharging them from the inn, but Gibbs politely asked him not to and instead asked the innkeeper to bring them both drinks on him. Curious to get back to their conversation, he responded to Eddie, "Now that I have bought you that drink, you can tell me who it is."

Holding his mug high as if making a toast, he uttered, "The witch!"

Not hearing his response because of the surrounding noise, he remarked, "I did not hear you. Who did you say it was?"

This time he shouted, drawing the attention of everyone around him, "The witch. She's the one who put the curse on the magistrate, killing him off, just as she did by giving those boys rabies."

Then Eddie's friend, who had been silent up to now, began to give his opinion, blaming Shawn for the killing, citing revenge as the motive. But the mayhem did not stop there. Before long, it escalated and grew into a frenzy, feeding on their hatred, pointing the finger at Isabel, blaming her for witchery and the evil eye. With the crowd becoming intensely rowdy, the shouts and cries for justice were all too much for Gibbs to bear. Losing his appetite, he was filled with disgust, and rising from his seat, he left for the solitude of his room, leaving Moore to handle things.

Retiring to his room, he reflected on the crowd's misbehavior, realizing there was a great resentment toward this one family. He wondered why they blamed Isabel for all the wrong that had happened in their town since tragedies, sicknesses, and accidents often happened to people all over. He also wondered why the locals considered her a witch. He understood from history that witchery was a thing of the past, where black magic was nothing more than the suspicious beliefs of fearful people. Persecuting people out of hate or robbing them of their property was usually the motive for proclaiming an individual as a witch or warlock. Towns such as these kept the old beliefs alive; hatred bred more hatred when the town lived in the past and never evolved into modern times.

Although they strongly believed Isabel was behind the contraction of rabies by the boys, it was hard for Gibbs to accept, seeing the incident as nothing more than an act of nature and categorizing it as an accident, which did not warrant an investigation. But because of the pressures from the locals with their ignorant ways of thinking, they would not hear of it and demanded justice just the same.

Gibbs was a modern man, and his reasoning was based on science and facts where all things had a simple explanation. This was the reason why witchery was long banished in the first place, to prevent such mobs from taking the law into their own hands and hanging innocent people whom they disliked. That's why when the crowd became rowdy and out of control, he had to get away, detesting those wild accusations, especially those of supernatural beliefs.

Sitting at the foot of his bed, he removed his shoes, tired from his long day. He knew he would have much to do in the next few days, busily interviewing all those associated one way or another with the magistrate. As he rested his head on the pillow, aimlessly staring at the ceiling, he hoped for a break in which he would get his first clue and find the underlying cause of this horrendous murder.

With the passing of several days, Gibbs and his partner were kept busy, as they had predicted. Although they had already conducted a great many interviews with associates of the magistrate, none was deemed beneficial to the case.

During this time, the boys' conditions grew worse, and they were affected by madness, acting like wild savages. They had now reached the second phase of the disease, and the sight of them was disgusting and depressing for their parents to witness. The rapid weight loss from not eating, foaming from the mouth with spasms of the jaw, accompanied by constant spitting and profuse sneezing was felt by the kin to be too much for a person to suffer. They consulted the town's clergy about their concerns and expressed their discontent. Something had to be done to prevent their children from such misery.

Tormented, many parents preferred mercy killing as a far better way to die rather than see this wretched disease eat away at the heart of their dignity. Although the Reverend Peterson did not agree with such killing, he felt it was in God's hands, not man's, but to satisfy them he accompanied them to the authorities in hopes that a more practical solution could be found. But as it was, the law was clear on the matter. Mercy killing was prohibited.

Disappointing as it was, nothing could be done to ease their pain. It was suggested that the parents stay away as the final end approached, for in doing so they would be spared the anguish and pain of watching their children's endless torment.

******

After uncovering nothing of significance in his investigation, Gibbs decided to give Isabel a visit that morning. Getting the directions from the local police, he and Inspector Moore took the fifteen-minute ride through the countryside. Though unfamiliar with the area, he was sure he had reached his destination when they passed a wrought iron arch that bore the family's insignia with bold letters, which read LAUGHTON ESTATE. Stopping before the main gate, which was supported by two pillars, he could not help notice five blackbirds all perched in a row on the arch. Whipping the horse's rear, he led the cart up the pathway leading to the mansion and stopped beneath the carriage porch. There Gibbs and Moore disembarked, looking about the stone mansion for a while before using the ring knocker to announce their presence.

Not long after, a tall man wearing a passive expression answered the door; standing motionless, he uttered not a sound. Finding it strange that he did not even question their presence, Gibbs instantly presented his credentials. Informing Dutch that he needed to speak with the lady of the house, they were allowed to enter into the hall and then led into the parlor where they awaited Isabel's appearance.

Within moments, she entered, greeted them with a big smile, and shook hands with both detectives as she made their acquaintance. She was a little pessimistic upon their arrival and wondered to what this unexpected visit was in reference. Motioning for them to sit by the fireplace, she politely offered them some tea while they spoke and sat across from them on her Chesterfield couch. After remarking how lovely her home was, Gibbs asked if she knew of the magistrate's death. Replying she did, she explained that while her son and Dutch were in town picking up provisions, they had heard of the awful ordeal that had taken place. Admitting she was shocked to hear of the death, she contended that she was even more surprised by the way he died, having had his eyes plucked out of his head.

"Plucked, you say?" Gibbs curiously asked.

"Yes, sort of. I meant his eyes were removed from their sockets," said Isabel, revising her statement.

At that moment, Dutch rolled in the serving table, bringing them their spot of tea. As he left the room, Gibbs commented on Dutch's social status, noting his silence, finding it peculiar that he had not heard him say a single word since they had entered the house.

"I doubt very much that you ever will. He was born a mute, most unfortunate for him," Isabel explained.

Redirecting his questions, Gibbs now turned to Isabel and stated that he had heard that Shawn was to be tried for assault and battery by the magistrate. Admitting it was true, she quickly added that he was falsely accused of the charges, and she could not wait to clear her son's name, believing he would be fully exonerated as soon as the next judge was appointed.

Gibbs wondered if Shawn was home, very much wanting to meet him and perhaps ask him a few questions. Not hesitating for even a moment, Isabel rang the servant's bell and informed Dutch to have Shawn come to the parlor so that he might meet the two detectives who wished to speak with him.

As they waited, Gibbs began to delve into Isabel's personal affairs, inquiring as to why she and her family were resented so much by the locals. Responding to his questions, she could only guess that perhaps it was jealousy over her wealth and power that separated her from the commoners. She knew that her family was disliked for many years, as far back as she could remember as a child and probably even further than that. Elaborating some more, she contended that they were considered an evil family and the town folk refused to associate themselves with them. Marked as a witch, she was unable to hire help to do repairs around the property and house. When it came to hiring workers, she had to employ outsiders from another town who knew nothing of the hate shown to them. Every misfortune that happened to someone was blamed on her, believing she had set upon them a spell or curse that overshadowed them. Lately, she seemed to get the blame for everything—the magistrate's death and was even thought to be responsible for the three boys contracting rabies.

"Just a misfortunate tragedy, and there in itself is the proof to show you how ridiculous the people around here all are," she concluded.

By this time, Shawn had entered the room, asking, as he walked over to the inspectors, if they were there to arrest him again.

Seeing the boy was obviously worried, Gibbs tried to put him at ease by replying, "No, no. Nothing like that. We have come here to have a friendly little chat and get a chance to make your acquaintance."

Inspectors Gibbs and Moore introduced themselves and shook hands with the lad who took the seat next to his mother. After indulging in friendly conversation for a few minutes, getting to know one another, Shawn felt more relieved when the inspector placed his cup back on the table, stating he did not want to take up any more of their time.

But before he left, Inspector Gibbs had one final question to ask Isabel, wanting to clear up something he had heard from the locals. Apologizing again for the intrusion of her privacy, he inquired about the past during the time of her mother when a few servants had died in her household. He asked if she knew anything of the mishaps, being that four women all had mysteriously met their deaths while under her parents' employment.

Remarking that she was a young child at the time, she admitted she did not know much of the situation. She did mention though that several deaths had occurred through accidents and an investigation had cleared her mother of any wrongdoing. Being the women were locals, it was another reason why the people had a great resentment toward her family. Blaming the deaths on witchery, they felt their wealth and power had influenced the outcome of the investigation and was the reason the law had exonerated her from the charges of murder.

Satisfied with her answers, Gibbs rose from his seat and thanked Isabel for the tea and wonderful chat. Explaining they would see themselves out, he and Moore exited the parlor and left by the front door. There to his amazement, he saw again the five blackbirds all perched on his carriage, and as he approached closer, they all flew away.

Moore took the reins as they returned to town, giving Gibbs the opportunity to contemplate on Isabel and her family. He felt Isabel was a sweet lady, and he was impressed by her honesty. He could not understand why the town's people held it against them as they did.

Though rather well built for a boy of fifteen, Shawn's mannerisms reflected the shyness of his innocence, and he felt Shawn was not capable of carrying out this sort of murder. Even though he was big and could easily overpower a person, he would still have had to have a strong stomach for a murder as gruesome as the magistrate's.

Of course, there was always the possibility that he could be wrong, but for now, he was more leery about Dutch and had serious reservations about him. Even if he were unable to speak, that would not impair his profile as a murderer. Rather broad shouldered and powerful, he did not seem to have a conscience. He could overpower a person, inflict serious damage, and not even have it bother him. Being tall in the saddle of a horse, he could have ridden up alongside of the magistrate, and being the right height, he could have easily pulled the magistrate's head back and struck repeatedly at his eyes.

Yet, as Gibbs thought further, he wondered what Dutch's motive would be. He actually did not have one, unless he was prompted by someone close to him and that would involve either Isabel or Shawn, but Gibbs could not get himself to believe that.

Still faced with the idea of Dutch, he knew it would be difficult for him to be interrogated under normal circumstances. Unable to speak and under the barrage of questions he would face, he would have to stop repeatedly in order for Dutch to write his responses on paper. This alone would lose the impact of a tense interrogation, and the breakdown to a confession would be lost. Nevertheless, no matter what the outcome, he did have to question Dutch eventually.

Chapter IX

Love Rekindled

Bored, now that Louise was no longer around, Shawn once again decided to accompany Dutch into town to pick up the needed provisions and supplies. Remembering well his last incident there, he felt safe from any additional threat imposed on him by the boys since they were now in confinement. However, if any conflict did arise, he would heed his mother's warnings and walk away from the trouble, inform Dutch of the situation, and bring the matter to the authorities immediately. He knew his mother was worried since she made him promise repeatedly and kept offering the same advice over and over again, something she did when she was anxious.

After a short, pleasant ride, they soon reached the general store and backed the wagon up against the loading platform. Dutch, as usual, went inside to double check on the order while Shawn remained outside, still sitting on the wagon.

Admiring the beautiful day, watching the birds in flight, he gazed about the area and noticed the familiarity of a girl whose back was toward him. Louise instinctively came to mind. He couldn't believe his eyes; she had come back. After all, she was the same height, shape, and had long, brown hair down her back. At that moment, all his emotions heightened. He recalled his past joy and how he longed again for that friendship he had once known. In an instant, it all came back, that look, her smile, and the laughter they had shared together in one harmony.

Feeling the flutter within his heart, he was exhilarated and jumped off the wagon, feeling a rush of adrenalin unleashed. Like a little boy out of control, he raced over to greet her while she stood conversing with two of her friends. Stopping behind her, he tapped her shoulder. As she turned to face him, he was flabbergasted. There was no rejoicing, excitement, or response of surprise as he had expected.

She looked at him with a blank expression, not having the faintest idea who he was. The happy smile he wore now turned to grief. Astounded by the turn of events, he was devastated and could not understand why she did not recognize him.

"Louise, it's me, Shawn!" he pitifully cried out.

Within that second, she opened her mouth and the sound of her voice was heard, but the words were not what he had expected to hear.

She kept repeating, "Do I know you?"

Stunned by her reaction, he was speechless for a brief moment, and once again, he tried to relate to her who he was, but it was to no avail, and her rejection hurt him even further. He felt at first she was playing a game, being the jokester she always was, but after her repeated denials and seeing her sincerity, he soon realized it was quite real.

Feeling she had had enough of this charade, she turned away.

Left alone and broken hearted, Shawn felt like a fool as he observed the girls giggling and glancing back as they departed. From a distance, one of them, a bit bubbly, turned to him, and smiling she shouted, "Her name is not Louise. It's Rachel, stupid." And soon as said, Rachel chased her friend where more of the frolicking and giggling continued.

With that response, he felt a little better, feeling he had at least been acknowledged and had gotten to know her name, although he did not get to know where she lived or any personal details of her life. Fooled by the contour of her eyes and the color of her hair, he found it remarkable how much she looked like Louise.

So preoccupied with Rachel and her friends, Dutch had completely slipped his mind, and he knew he was probably wondering where he was. Racing back, as predicted, Dutch had been worried half to death by his absence. Waiting intensely on the platform, he had already loaded the entire order onto the wagon by himself. Noticing Shawn's approach, his expression changed dramatically. He no longer had that distressed look which he had worn earlier. Nevertheless, Shawn could see that Dutch was not at all pleased by what he had done. Not wanting to infuriate him any more, he apologized and sheepishly slipped into the cart, never mentioning a word of his encounter.

Late in the afternoon of the following day, there was a rapid pounding of the knocker on the front door. Shawn, who happened to be nearby, answered it, shocked by whom he saw. There, standing before him, was Rachel.

Nervously, she fiddled with her hair as she expressed sorrow for having to bother him. Noticeably upset, she began to explain her ordeal. While riding on the main road with her friend, her horse had gone lame. Not knowing what else to do, she tied him to a tree, and she and her friend followed the path that led to the house, seeking help.

Shawn eagerly responded that it was no trouble at all and asked for a moment while he hitched a wagon for them all to return to her carriage. Upon arriving, he unhitched her horse and walked the animal around to determine which foot was lame. Seeing all four of its legs were perfectly fine, the notion suddenly struck him that this was just an excuse to meet him. Playing along with Rachel's game, he remarked, "Ah, yes. One of his shoes was loose." Taking the hammer from his toolbox, he tapped the shoe lightly a couple of times, announcing, "That should solve your problem."

Rachel was thrilled, and the smile upon her face reflected her sure delight. She was in love with Shawn from the moment she had set eyes upon him and had to make his acquaintance by using any excuse. Although she was nine months older than he was, it did not seem to matter, and soon they became friends and began to share intimate moments.

Rachel's family was also rich, and both families were well

acquainted with one another, having been old rivals in business. A long time ago, during their grandparents' time, the rivalry had begun. They had been in the shipping industry, and their fierce competition for cargo had caused such a stir between the two companies that it created an atmosphere of bad blood. Eventually Isabel's father, after inheriting the family business, grew tired of the pressures involved and decided to sell the company. Spitefully, he would not give in and sell to the Thompsons, even though they had offered more, but instead held out and sold his interest to a Northern Ireland company for much less.

This infuriated them. Feeling that they had dealt fairly with the price they offered, the Laughtons' disrespectful, contemptuous behavior could not be forgiven, making a bad relationship far worse.

But despite their differences and their family's hatred toward one another, their love affair flourished, and they secretly met at Shawn's estate, hidden away from all eyes except their own.

Chapter X

At Death's Doorway

While Shawn was developing his new love affair, Nancy, his biological mother, had decided she wanted her son back.

Uninterested for fifteen years, being young and full of spirit, she had no desire for motherhood nor to be tied down with a child so early in her life. However, now a mature woman of thirty-four, unmarried, and having nothing to show in her life, the passage of time had spurred a change of heart. With many years to reconsider her wrongs and regrets, she realized her life was empty and her future was bleak, and in her discontent, she was prompted by visions of reconciliation with her son. Shawn was the only thing she had left.

Aware that fifteen years was a very long time, what would be the repercussions if she came back into his life? What a foolish mistake she had made! An unforgivable one! And if Shawn felt that way, she would accept the consequences and never bother him again. She yearned to know what had become of him, how he looked, and if he was happy. She wanted this one opportunity to reconcile with him and perhaps to have his forgiveness, which she so desperately needed. Not that she deserved his forgiveness, but she held out for that little chance of hope that he might find it within his heart to do so. Tormented daily, she relived that awful day and the moment she turned her back on him. She was hurt and felt genuine remorse for what she had done, not so much for herself, but for her son. She should not have waited so long to get him back. Now grown and almost a man, she had missed out on all those wonderful moments of his childhood. Wiping his tears when he was sad, watching him grow, and comforting him with a mother's love was a treasure and memory lost in time, and she knew they could never be regained. She had deprived herself of golden years and smiles from memorable thoughts that would have been so precious. Instead, only one memory burned deep in her mind and that was that she had given up her son. She was so ashamed; she didn't even know his name.

Peggy, who had felt this way for a long time, was glad to see that her daughter had finally come around. For the first time in a long time, they agreed on something and wanted to rectify this terrible mistake. Making this decision together, Peggy, a grandmother, did not need much convincing. Deciding to talk with Isabel alone, she was well aware that Isabel was not going to greet her with open arms and turn over the boy after raising him for fifteen years. After all, Isabel thought of Shawn as her son, and Peggy knew that. She also knew that the situation was volatile and could get very ugly with Isabel not wishing to be the least bit cooperative.

Peggy was a little afraid to approach Isabel. In matters such as these, the outcome would be serious enough when talking to an ordinary person, but when confronting a witch, the results could be deadly. Therefore, she chose to go alone to protect her daughter from any repercussions Isabel might take.

Peggy did not choose to meet Isabel in the dead of the night as she had some fifteen years ago when she left the baby on the doorstep. She preferred the security of the day when she felt safer, announcing her presence as she knocked upon the door early that very morning.

Dutch, who usually was the one to answer the door, did not do so on this particular occasion, but instead Isabel did. She somehow expected this visit was to come and wanted to confront Peggy one-to-one. As

Isabel opened the door, there they stood face to face, and her expression was enough to show Peggy that she was not at all welcomed. Isabel had no intentions of inviting her into the house; her very presence there that morning made Isabel angry, sure of the reason why Peggy had come in the first place.

Before Peggy could say a word, Isabel rudely interrupted her, wasting no time to criticize. "What do you want? You know you have no business coming here."

"I was hoping to have a word with you about the boy," Peggy implored.

"You mean Shawn?"

"Is that what you named him?"

"I am not interested in talking about it. I don't care the least bit to know or hear what you have to say," Isabel answered, not in the mood for idle chitchat.

The situation already bad enough, she had no desire to flair up or anger Isabel. After all, she was petrified and felt her life hung in the midst. Preferring the peaceful approach, not wanting to appear overly assertive or make an issue out of her visit, Peggy begged, "Please, just give me a moment. I know I don't deserve it, but for Shawn's sake, hear me out."

"For his sake, I will. Not for yours!" Isabel exclaimed. "You know, I truly don't believe you people! After all these years, now you want to talk. Why didn't you think about it before you abandoned him? Then you wouldn't have had to come here today and stir trouble."

"I never meant to, but as a mother, you can understand how I feel. My daughter is very upset, and I need to help her. Wouldn't you do the same for your child?" Peggy pleaded, hoping to appeal to Isabel's maternal instinct.

Not showing the least bit of respect for Peggy, Isabel lashed back, "I definitely would not be in that situation in the first place. I never would have abandoned him! He was so beautiful. A perfect boy! Healthy and full of life! And you just tossed him away as if he was a piece of trash. I could spit in your face!"

Peggy could feel the tension swell between them, but determined as she was, she pressed on. "You're right. I deserve your anger," she acknowledged, trying to look humble. "You have done a wonderful job of raising him. Of that, we have no doubt. But there is a difference between us. You, being wealthy, money is not a problem. But when you live a life of poverty, having no money, or food to fill your cupboards, things are bad when you have to struggle from day to day, not knowing when your next meal is going to be. That's why we have done this," Peggy explained, mixing truth with lies and falling short of the true reason for the abandonment. "We didn't have the means to raise a child. His life would have been shrouded with nothing but despair."

"So now you suddenly have money and food? This is what you are trying to tell me?" Isabel questioned.

"No, it's not because of that. It's because we've realized our wrong for a long time. We want to make it up to him and have him back. We are his rightful family—you know, his flesh and blood—and my daughter is his mother."

"Correction! I'm his mother," Isabel shot back. "Your daughter is not his mother. She's just the woman who gave birth to him. I'm the only mother he has ever known or will ever need. I was the one who wiped his tears, not Nancy. I was the one who stood up all night when he was sick, not Nancy. I was the one who reassured him when he was frightened, not Nancy. How dare you call her his mother? You have no right—no right at all!"

"I admit my daughter has done much wrong in her life, but she's trying to turn her life around. It wasn't her fault. It was mine. I'm the one who took him and put him on your doorstep. Why should she be punished?"

"I'm not trying to punish her. I just don't feel any sympathy toward her misfortunes. Let's be frank! Your daughter is a prostitute and a drunk, and she didn't want to be tied down and raise a child. If she was any mother worth calling a mother, she would have gotten work, decent work, and slave on her hands and knees, if need be, to earn her money and sacrifice for him. But she chose to be what she is—a drunken slut. Did you actually believe I was going to give him up just like that without a fight? What were you thinking?"

"Well, we hoped you would have understood why we had done it and why we so desperately want him back now."

"Listen, let's get one thing straight! YOU left him on my doorstep. On that night, you changed his future! All our futures! Shawn does not need you now. He has me as his mother. There is no way you will get him back. So for yours and your daughter's sake, I say forget the past and live for tomorrow. As far as I'm concerned, the matter is over. So I suggest you leave now while the going is good and never return," Isabel warned, and with that final declaration, she slammed the door in Peggy's face, ending any further debate.

Peggy could see that the conversation was over and not much more could be said to her advantage. Perhaps Isabel was right, she pondered. Maybe, for Shawn's sake, she should let it go. Now all she had to do was convince Nancy.

But apparently, the debate was not ended. When Peggy returned home unsuccessful in her venture, Nancy blew into a rage. Bitterly, she argued her point with her mother, "Who does she think she is? I am the birth mother, and she can't stop me from taking my son back! Why did you give in so easily? I knew I should have come with you. You never do anything right."

Feeling she could not hide the truth any longer, Peggy confessed, "I never mentioned this before but the reason why I refused to tell you who it was, was not to keep the information from you, but it was because the person who has your son is a witch."

Appalled by what she had just heard, Nancy screeched, "You left my son to a witch? Whatever possessed you to do such a thing? What are you stupid? Of all the people in town, you left him to her. This is even more reason why I have to get him back."

"You have to understand, Nancy, you are not dealing with an ordinary person," Peggy cautioned. "When you confront a witch, you don't anger them. The consequences could be deadly."

"So that's why you gave in so easily!" Nancy chided. "If you're so afraid of her, why did you leave him with her in the first place? I don't understand."

"You know why—we've been all through this before. You weren't married and what you were doing was sinful, and I felt by doing this, I was putting evil where evil belonged."

"Are you saying my son is evil?"

"Nancy, now you're twisting my words. I don't know what I was thinking at the time. But I....I just did it," she stammered. "Maybe I acted impulsively. But I felt the unclean birth was against God."

"Ma, you are so pathetic!" Nancy said, throwing her arms up in frustration. "You know what you are? You're a fanatic, a religious fanatic!"

Not wanting to fight anymore, Peggy gave in. "Maybe so, but getting your son back isn't going to be as easy as you think. You just don't walk into someone's life after fifteen years and look to take away her son. Remember, she loves him, and God knows how far she would go to keep him. That family has a reputation of witchery. Many deaths have occurred in that household, and I don't wish to be another."

"Well, you don't have to worry about your precious life," Nancy said condescendingly. "I'll be handling it from now on, and I'm certainly not frightened of her. One way or another, I'll get my son back, witch, or no witch!"

From the look in Nancy's eyes to the tone of her statement, Peggy became alarmed. "What are you planning to do? I want to know. You're beginning to frighten me!"

Confidently, Nancy threatened, "She could either give him up peacefully or be exposed in court before the public, showing she is not the true mother, something I believe she would be very much against. After all, I have the law on my side."

The bickering continued for some time. Although Peggy tried her best to dissuade Nancy, nothing she said could convince her differently. She had always been strong minded. Young and feisty, she was full of fight. Come tomorrow, she planned to return with her mother, but this time, she insisted on doing the negotiating.

******

As morning broke, Nancy, along with her mother, did keep her engagement as promised and soon reached the Laughtons' estate. On their way there, Peggy was visibly shaken, nervous about the confrontation her daughter might have with Isabel. Over and over, she implored Nancy to be diplomatic.

However, this time their visit was warmly received as Isabel answered the door and welcomed them in with open arms. "Please forgive my rudeness to your mother the other day. After giving it considerable thought, I felt guilty over my behavior and how inappropriately I acted. I realize how offensive I must have sounded and how insensitive I was toward your concerns. I am actually glad you came back so that I can retract my earlier views."

Stunned, hesitating a moment before answering, Peggy remarked, "Actually, we are rather shocked. We never anticipated this sort of reception."

"Well, in any case, since you are here, please come in and we can discuss this matter civilly over a cup of tea." From the hall, Isabel led them into the parlor. Stopping before the fireplace, she invited them to sit on the sofa and warm up a bit. She then turned and placed herself across from them, sitting in her favorite armchair.

Cordially, she smiled at Nancy as she expressed her concern, "I believe we should address this matter in a delicate way. If there is going to be a transaction, I would like to know what sort of arrangement you had in mind."

Not having one, Nancy bluntly responded, raising her voice slightly, "I don't need one since I, as the real mother, have a legal claim to my son. I am prepared to bring this before a court of law if you do not wish to give him up."

"Well, suppose I don't agree," Isabel challenged.

Not intimidated in the least, Nancy stood firm, as she threatened, "You don't have a choice. You know you will lose if I pursue this!"

"I see. Do you have a birth certificate from a midwife to substantiate your claim?"

"No, I did not have the assistance of a midwife. I was lucky to give birth on my own."

Out of curiosity, Isabel fished for more answers, "Then I assume you recorded the birth yourself at the town hall."

"No," she replied, "there was no need to at the time since we no longer had the baby. But I do have witnesses that can verify my claim, and their testimony would help prove I gave birth. They are also aware of the abandonment and that the child you have is indeed mine."

Very interested now, Isabel questioned, "And who would that be?"

"My mother, two friends I am affiliated with in town, and the Pastor Peterson," she rambled. "They all know of Shawn's true identity. All of them would be willing to testify on my behalf, if need be," she arrogantly boasted. "So I'm sure we can avoid any further delay and get this all over with today."

As silence prevailed, neither said a word for a few moments while Isabel reflected on the situation, finding her back against the wall. She suspected that if this issue was brought before the court, Nancy would probably win, and that would mean she would lose Shawn, a risk she could not afford to take. She was also worried over Shawn's emotions and wanted to spare him any hardship that might result from a bitter exchange. The mere presence of Nancy, along with her aggressiveness, offended her. She resented her ill manners, especially her persistence, and was outraged at the thought of how she expected her to disregarded fifteen years of love and devotion in a moment's notice. It was obvious that she was callous, and there was no way she was going to turn her son over to this bitch.

Breaking the silence finally, Nancy began, "Listen. We've wasted enough time. I want to see my son. Where is he? Is he here?"

Using the term "my son" really got Isabel fuming for beneath that composed look she wore, she could feel her blood boiling like a fiery volcano ready to erupt. Calmly and playing the role to the fullest, Isabel turned and picked up the servant's bell she used to summon Dutch. As he approached, Isabel rose from her chair and asked him to have Shawn come directly into the parlor, but by the piercing stare in Isabel's eyes, he became aware at the insinuation in her look that he was to ignore her request.

"I don't believe there will be any need for a court intervention," she said reassuringly. "I'm positive this matter can be promptly handled between us. I am really concerned about Shawn's welfare since he is in the middle. It would be less stressful if we settle this quietly and peacefully without public view." Smiling and looking bubbly now, Isabel turned to her guests and remarked, "I hope you will both join me in a spot of tea. Then we can discuss in detail how we should go about this." Stating she would only be a moment, she walked briskly into the kitchen.

Isabel was barely out of earshot when Nancy turned to her mother and began, "See I told you! She knows I'm in my right! And you were afraid. I showed her…"

But before she could finish her statement, Peggy interrupted, "Shhh! What's the matter with you? She's going to hear you!"

Unafraid, Nancy got up from her chair and began to look around the room. Her curiosity was heightened by a small box on the table next to the armchair. As she reached to pick it up, Peggy warned, almost in a whisper, "Nancy, put that down! Isabel will be back any minute!"

"Oh Ma, stop it! You're always so afraid of everything," Nancy said irreverently. Disregarding her mother's warnings, she opened the lid and peeked in the box. Seeing a gold medal on a chain, she turned the medal over and read the inscription aloud, *To Shawn, Love, Your Mother.*

Isabel had intended to give this present to her son to remind him of how special he was to her. It was not because of his birthday or some special occasion she did this, but it was because of how she felt, wanting to express her love and devotion. She knew it was the foolish sentiments of a mother, but she could not help feeling that when he wore it, he would be carrying her close to his heart. Loving him as she did was beyond all words, and she wanted him to have something with which to remember her and had felt this was the most appropriate way.

Jealously, Nancy removed the medal from its casing, "Can you believe this? I'll show her! Mother, indeed!" Never having experienced a mother-son relationship first hand, she was determined to make sure Shawn would not get this medal, enviously denying Isabel the right to be called Mother.

Not realizing she had broken the chain in her fury, she quickly slipped it into her pocket and put the empty box back in its rightful place just seconds before Isabel returned, rolling in the tea on the serving table. Pushing it across the room to where they sat, she filled three cups from the silver kettle, boasting that this tea was a special blend and was carefully guarded in her family for its unique quality and good flavor.

As they drank, Peggy remarked on its fine taste. The grin on Isabel's face sealed their fate, and being only a minute or so before it took its effect, they soon realized how treacherous she really was. Although Isabel drank the tea as well, their suspicions were never aroused, giving little thought to the awful pains that suddenly struck them in the pits of their stomachs. At first, a crash of a cup was heard as it hit the floor, splattering it into numerous pieces, followed by the hard thump of a body that fell simultaneously.

Nancy, gasping for air, curled in a fetal position, looked up at Isabel, trying to ask that fatal question why. Across from where Isabel stood, was Peggy, slumped back on the couch, dying quickly; she did not utter a sound or even know what had hit her. Having a contorted expression, eyes bulged, mouth wide, she wore an image of pure and sheer shock.

How could they have known she had an ulterior motive for asking them in? So sweet and charming, she had planned and executed her devious plot to the peak of perfection, both unaware they were to die.

Fulfilled with the pleasure of sure contempt, Isabel, tipping her head slightly, swooned over the bodies that lay before her. Never having used it before, she was very surprised to see how well and quickly it worked.

Just then, Dutch returned alone. Well aware of the delicate situation, he was not surprised by the dead bodies in the living room since Isabel had taken him into her confidence before executing her plan.

Isabel had insisted on serving the tea herself since she had found the poison some time ago that had belonged to her mother and which she suspected had been used to murder the women servants. However, before serving her guests, she had wisely added the antidote, which would spare the painful cramps and quick, agonizing death, to her cup of tea.

Now the only thing left to do was to dispose of the bodies before Shawn returned home. She did not want to be faced with questions and have to explain the tragedies, which had just taken place. She knew for the moment he was occupied with Rachel somewhere on the property and would not be home until late in the afternoon.

She was well aware of their love affair and what was going on. Even though they felt they had deluded the world around them, they certainly did not fool mother, and as long as Shawn was content, so was Isabel, never giving him the slightest indication that she knew.

Isabel was concerned and needed to eliminate all, if any, suspicion of poisoning. She planned to divert attention and make it appear as if the tragic actions were that of a raving maniac. Dutch bound their hands behind their backs and tied a short rope around each of their necks using his powerful hands to tighten the loops, making the murders appear to be from strangulation. Since the women had walked to Isabel's home, there was no need to get rid of their transportation, making matters much easier.

Bringing the flat wagon around to the back of the mansion, the two women were placed in the bed of the cart and covered from sight by two horse blankets. Dutch, following Isabel's strict orders, waited until nightfall before he left to dispose of the bodies. By then Shawn was having dinner with his mother who had made excuses for Dutch's absence by claiming that he was not feeling well that evening and had retired to his room earlier.

While they enjoyed their dinner, Dutch, as instructed, was on the road searching for a good place to ditch the bodies. He needed a place that was secluded and safe from prying eyes. Knowing the area quite well, he stopped along the roadside where the river was parallel to the road. Deciding this was the perfect place to dump the bodies, he used the steep decline to roll them down the embankment, landing at the water's edge. His fears of being seen allayed, he breathed a sigh of relief. Then he returned home as if nothing had happened.

Chapter XI

Last Rights

At dawn of that misty day, there was an uncontrollable pounding on the chapel door of the town's parish. Mary Hopkins, whose eyes were swollen and red from sobbing profusely, felt distressed by the most dreadful news she had ever received.

She had just been informed of the deaths of the boys, and closest to her heart, her own son. Although she knew her son was affected by paralytic rabies, she had never suspected his death would be so sudden. Perhaps it was best it happened this way, she contended; he would suffer no more, and his soul would finally be at peace. Needing spiritual comfort and not having anyone else to turn to, she sought out Reverend Peterson for help in her hour of desperation.

Undeniably, the three boys had all met horrific deaths. Now that the last one had died, the parents of each of them were notified, and they were all asked to meet at ten in the morning by the old mill. After witnessing a brief ceremony of last rites, the place would be set ablaze. Harsh as it was, due to health risks, this cremation would mark the final resting place for their children.

Their cries of grief expressed their deep emotions as Reverend

Peterson began to administer the comforting words of last rites. Calling out the names of their sons, two of the parents, unable to bear the strain, rushed toward the old mill, wanting to set their eyes on their loved ones a final time. The authorities, forbidding this action, intervened quickly and suppressed the women from going any further, hoping to spare them any more hardship. Meekly, they offered no resistance.

"It is best that they are remembered as they were," the Reverend Peterson proclaimed. "Dying from such a wretched disease is a sight unsuitable for any mother to see."

Not wanting to prolong the agony any longer than necessary, the reverend immediately signaled for the funeral to get on its way. With oil drums, the old mill was doused with the flammable liquid, and the torches were lit and held ready for the command to ignite the structure. As the passage of the dead was read by the reverend, the signal was given for the torches to be thrown. It was only a matter of seconds before the old mill lit like a match as the aged timber burst into a fiery ball of flames. With the structure being the inferno that it was, the heat was so intense that it forced the congregation back. It was all too much for the mothers to bear, and their faces etched in sorrow, they watched the flames burn rampant. In their final moments of grief, two of the three women were overpowered by the swells of weakness and trauma, collapsing from their anguish.

Nearby to offer the frail women a helping hand were Inspectors Gibbs and Moore. Sympathetically, they raised the women to their feet, giving each a supporting arm and a firm embrace, along with a few words of encouragement to be strong. Realizing that the children had undergone an awful ordeal, been cheated out of life, and were sorely missed, they tried to reach out to the parents by extending their sincerest condolences.

It was some time before the cinders cooled; nevertheless, the parents remained patiently to the very end. For their final action, they scooped some of the cremated remains of the departed and held it close to their hearts, forever remembering this day and their loved ones.

Chapter XII

The Arrest

It was not until the second day after the cremation that the bodies of Nancy and Peggy were discovered in the river. Two youngsters who were fishing had been looking for the perfect spot to cast their lines when they stumbled across the partly submerged bodies of the two women. The boys, excited over their unexpected find, raced immediately into town, notifying the authorities.

Inspectors Gibbs and Moore, first to respond to the scene, pulled the women out of the river and placed them onto a white sheet along the bank's edge. After a quick inspection of Nancy, Gibbs observed that her wrists were bound and death appeared to be from strangulation.

Searching through her pockets, he discovered the medal that Isabel had intended to give Shawn as a gift. Placing his glasses on so that he could get a better look, he observed that the engraving expressed a special sentiment that read, *To Shawn, Love, Your Mother.* Putting the medal with the broken chain in his pocket, he held it for evidence.

Inspector Moore concluded Peggy's death to have more or less the same pattern as Nancy's and was most anxious to return to the mortuary where they could conduct a more thorough postmortem examination. Once the women were transferred by cart, Doctor Lane would officially be responsible and would perform the pre-examination with the assistance of Inspector Gibbs.

Gibbs, who had earlier suspected strangulation, now had second thoughts about his theory after removing their bondage. His suspicions were aroused as he inspected their wrists, which did not show any rope burns, bruises, or abrasions to their skin, and he deemed this lack of wounds to be very strange. Deep into the examination, his curiosity intensified. He noted the eye sockets had not swelled, nor did the vessels on the sclera burst within the eye. The simple facts deluded him, and as he continued the examination, he discovered there was no fracture to the hyoid bone. Positioned just behind the tongue, this was usually the case when brutal force was applied to the neck, establishing the proof he needed.

Their deaths were definitely not consistent with the pattern of wounds found in strangulation. As he probed further, he did not see blue lips indicating lack of oxygen to the brain; this too he felt was also extremely suspicious. An autopsy would clearly establish if strangulation was a cause of death, showing a burst heart, verifying that indeed it was.

Nevertheless, as it stood for now, from what he had already observed, he was pretty much convinced of the contrary. He concluded that they were already dead when bound, meaning someone deceptively wanted their deaths to appear to look different than the actual murder. Whatever the unknown origin of death truly was, he was sure that an autopsy would shed new light.

For the moment, he reflected on the magistrate's death and wondered if the two incidents were connected in any way. Was it possible, he contemplated, that the same person who had murdered the magistrate had also killed the women? Although there were dissimilarities between the two types of murders, it did not entirely rule out a murderer's profile or his pattern. That could easily change according to the encounter and his surroundings.

After all, he did have a potential suspect for now, and reaching deep into his pocket, he removed the medal with its broken chain, staring once again at the shiny medallion. Gibbs felt that it was very probable that during Nancy's final moments in her struggle for life, she may have ripped the chain off the killer's neck without being noticed and held onto it to incriminate her attacker. Whether this was the actual reason why she had possession of the medal remained uncertain. There were still many questions unanswered, and since the medal did belong to Shawn, that alone was cause enough to arrest him on suspicion of murder.

Early the following morning, the paddy wagon pulled up to the Laughtons' estate. Gibbs and Moore, along with two constables, were at the front entrance waiting for a response after having pounded forcefully on the door. Isabel, who was having breakfast in the solarium, was close enough to hear the voice of Inspector Gibbs as he spoke to Dutch, inquiring about Shawn's presence.

With the paddy wagon parked out front and a heavy police escort in the hall, she began to worry and questioned Gibbs as to the meaning of this intrusion. From inside his jacket pocket he removed a long folded paper and handed it to Isabel as he stated that it was a warrant for Shawn's arrest.

"Arrest?" she questioned, looking a bit bewildered and confused.

Opening the contents of the warrant, she suddenly felt a weakness come over her, reading that her son was suspected of murder. Overly excited, Isabel felt a rush of heat rise to her face and bellowed out, "I cannot believe this is true!"

Gibbs, offering some insight to the circumstances, explained about the medal and that he would have to take Shawn into custody for a few days for questioning, adding that this sort of arrest was nothing more than routine, although that didn't make Isabel feel any better.

As her desperation swelled, Isabel, triggered by motherly instinct, came to her son's defense. She knew well in her heart that Shawn was being falsely accused for something she had done. Curiously, she questioned, "What medal were you referring to?"

Reaching into his pocket, removing the medal, he held it out before Isabel's face, and replied, "This medal with both your names engraved on it."

Her face became flushed with shock. She instantly recognized it, and trying to hide her guilt, she quickly responded, "Where did you say you found it?"

While providing an explanation, he gave little details of the crime scene and only specified that it had been found inside Nancy's sweater pocket. Until now, she had no idea that the medal had even been missing.

She was in a predicament. She could not allow herself to stand idly by and let Shawn take the blame for her actions. She dreaded the thought of having him put back into that filthy cell and could not forgive herself if it happened to him again. She knew she had to act quickly, be shrewd, decisive, and most of all very careful of what she said. Desperately, she tried her best to obscure the truth and draw away any suspicion. She had to be convincing enough not to give Gibbs the slightest indication of doubt toward her story.

Arguing on her son's behalf, she claimed that this could not be possible. Offering an explanation, she assured Gibbs that the medal was indeed stolen and she was able to show him proof. Insisting that he follow her, she led the way into the parlor and took him straight to the table next to her favorite armchair. Picking up the small box, she shoved it at his face, and quickly opening it, she bluntly said, "You see. It's empty and it was right from here that it was taken."

Not saying a word, Isabel could see from the expression on his face that Gibbs was not at all impressed by her display of proof. She felt he required more and reasoned that he should know why Peggy and Nancy had come to the house in the first place. Further manipulating the facts to her advantage, Isabel masked the truth as she expressed her need for more servants, lying that she had interviewed both of them several days ago for positions as a cook and housemaid. Establishing that Nancy had both the means and motive to take it, she believed that the medal must have been stolen during her absence while preparing tea, and since the medal was pure gold, Nancy could not resist the temptation.

Gibbs could not help feeling that Isabel was protecting her son. After years of being a detective, Gibbs' skill of observation was highly trained, and he could see in her eyes and how she conducted herself that she was not at all telling the truth. After all, Isabel was never a good liar, and Gibbs saw right through her, knowing that she would do anything to prevent her son's arrest.

He almost felt guilty for what he had to do, knowing he had to disappoint her and take Shawn into custody, even if it would break her heart. Though he felt she was a sweet woman, he could not allow himself to get involved in his personal feelings. He had to focus on the crime, be true toward his principles, and above all, faithful to his duty, regardless of his emotions. Expressing his regrets, he explained he was still going to take Shawn in for questioning. He assured her that he would be easy on the boy and make his stay as painless as possible.

Dutch was then instructed to have Shawn come down from his room and meet them in the hall. Upon their return, Shawn, puzzled, looked at his mother, searching for an explanation. He had no idea why he was being arrested.

Embracing Shawn, she touched his face gently on the cheek and gave him a kiss, and although she told him not to worry, she could not hold back the tears. She promised him that he would be out soon, and come heaven or hell, she meant every word. As they cuffed and escorted him into the paddy wagon, Isabel sobbed even more. She could not forget the pitiful look in his eyes as he gazed out through the barred window as they departed.

******

On this early morning, Rachel too had sensed something was terribly wrong. Like every morning, she waited for Shawn in the forest under a willow tree that was their favorite hideaway. After a considerable amount of time had passed and he still was nowhere to be found, she grew concerned. This was not like him; he had never missed a day of their meeting. Worried, she decided to stop by his home to see for herself the cause of his delay. To her surprise, she learned of Shawn's arrest as Isabel, who was deeply distressed, could not hold back the tears of her grief.

In haste, Rachel dashed off, snapping the whip to her team of horses and raced a path straight for the jail. Excitedly, she confronted Inspector Gibbs and implored him to release Shawn, pouring out her deepest concerns about his incarceration. She knew well in her heart he was innocent and could not have committed such a heinous crime. She felt it was her obligation to bring this matter to his attention, declaring herself as a witness, attesting that it was virtually impossible for Shawn to have killed those women, considering he had been with her every day for the past four weeks. Most certainly, she assured Gibbs, this arrest had to be a mistake. Shawn was not at all the raving monster he was seeking. To her, he was the sweetest person she had ever met, and she knew that he was incapable of hurting anyone.

At this point, it was quite obvious to Gibbs that Rachel was madly in love with Shawn, and her purpose was to protect him at all costs. Nevertheless, he was still considered the prime suspect for now, and he had to follow up with the questioning in order to gather the facts and draw his own conclusions. He could not say by one's characteristics, he was a mild mannered man and harmless, for he saw for himself the two halves of a mad mind that could fool the best of detectives.

Despite all of Rachel's pleas, Gibbs had no choice but to deny her as he assured her that if indeed Shawn turned out to be innocent, he would be released sooner than she expected.

For the most part, Rachel's testimony had done more harm than good. Her love for Shawn had cost her dearly; their secret rendezvous over the past few weeks were now exposed. She had no way of knowing the damage she had now created. Their secret immediately became the talk of local gossipers. Like in all small towns, the news spread quickly, and by nightfall, even her family had caught wind of their secret relationship. Furious over the revelation, they felt their daughter had betrayed their trust and dishonored their dignity.

******

By the very least, this day of pain and despair was far from over. Isabel, who had been restless for most of the morning, was troubled by the arrest and had to find a way to quickly remedy this problem. She had promised her son that his stay in jail would not be long. After all, she had given him her word, and by no means would she disappoint him, even if she had to resort to witchery. She was desperate and had to find a way to free him.

Leaving her parlor, she began to climb the steps to her attic where she could have the solitude of silence. It was here in this room where her best thoughts came. Sitting in her armchair, leaning back comfortably, she gazed out of the terrace doors, meditating over a solution for Shawn's arrest. Feeling much was at stake, she could not afford to fail him now. Whatever she conspired, it would have to have an impact and be effective enough to draw blame elsewhere so that the evidence would be overwhelming and have him released. Heavy-hearted, she was consumed with many thoughts and realized that if it had not been for Peggy and Nancy's deaths, her son would not be in jail at this moment. While mulling over many scenarios, she was struck with the most brilliant of ideas, and the answer could not have been more clear. She concluded, since the deaths of two women were responsible for her son's incarceration, the deaths of two more women would ultimately free him. It was all so simple.

Pleased with herself, she felt less pressured. She never knew how capable she was of concocting such a well-planned diversion. This scheme was so clever that she would be able to kill two birds with one stone. She would now have the opportunity, as well as the pleasure, of silencing Nancy's friends who knew too much of Shawn's identity, and at the same time, their deaths would give Gibbs the impression that the killer was still at large, freeing her son.

For the moment, the Reverend Peterson posed no threat; having no immediate need for him to meet his maker for now, she would dispense with him later. For the time being, the women were high on her list of priorities, and she would deal with them first. Still prostitutes and actively trying to attract customers, they would be easy prey for the plan that she had in mind for them.

Chapter XIII

The Greek God Apollo

As night approached, the weekend as always attracted a houseful of guests at the Rocklin Inn. Taking advantage of a gathering such as this, Nancy's friends were out as usual, venturing to catch the attention of potential customers. With the night young, the hook was baited for an enthusiastic catch, trying to entice the roaming eye with the sheerness of silk stockings and sexy, low-cut dresses. The ladies of the night with their persuading smiles were sampling their fine goods to any lustful person who could afford to pay the initial fee for an evening of fun and excitement.

Screeching its wheels as it came to a halt, a coach pulled up and one lone passenger stepped out. Walking through the doors, he paused before an atmosphere filled with smoke and the hubbub of many loud voices as he looked over the interior of the inn. Those who were near took little notice of his presence and continued with their enjoyable activities.

Crossing the room, he set his sights on Nancy's two friends who were sitting alone in private conversation enjoying a drink, although business was not at all as anticipated. Like a magnet, he was drawn to their table, and being six foot four, he looked down upon them, flashing his wicked, little grin. Having a pencil-thin moustache and sharply dressed, looking especially dapper in his two-tone shoes, he was indeed a quick eye for any woman who was out on the prowl. With fair complexion outlined by his tightly slicked-back dark hair, he wore blue tinted, wire-rimmed glasses, which also added to his already attractive, sharp features.

He soon became a real interest to the two women who found him to be very appealing. Never having seen him before, they were instantly infatuated by his charisma as he smiled, exchanged greetings, and asked to be seated at their table. He had a magical power of persuasion, and they found his seduction equally irresistible. He wasted no time getting to the point and removed a roll of money the size of a fist from his pocket. Finding him most generous, his hospitality overwhelmed them as he offered to buy them both a round of drinks. Rubbing his shoulders and curling his hair between their fingertips, they showered him with attention. As the waitress returned with their drinks, he shot a wink at her and pulled out his roll of money again. Their eyes glued to his currency, he enticed them by peeling off a pound and impressed the waitress with a sizable tip by tossing a half a crown on her tray.

Believing they had found the catch of the night, they made their moves, getting up close and well acquainted. It was not long before the mood accelerated, and with an insinuation of an unorthodox proposition, his request was accepted. They were surprised that he was prepared to pay dearly for an orgy with both women. Finding this special request to be their first, these women, who shared their room on a rotation basis, were now confronted with the embarrassment of their own nakedness before one another in the same bed. But what the hell, they contended. He was willing to pay very well for a good time, and they would soon get over their uneasiness once payment was received.

Leaving their surroundings for seclusion and privacy, the women led the way, taking their rich client up to their room. Striking a match after entering the darkness, she lit a candle and walked across the room, transferring the flame to a second candle on the table near the bed. Walking to the vanity, she placed the candle before the mirror, briefly gazing at her reflection. It was then that Elaine quickly turned and demanded the payment of the two pounds in advance before any pleasure was to be performed.

After being cheated several times, she made it a policy to collect payment before pleasure was rendered. Although feeling it was a bit expensive, he did not debate the matter and paid her what was expected, plus a crown more for a bottle of wine. He wanted this evening to be well remembered, and he asked her to be good enough to fetch the wine for him to induce his excitement and pleasure. Agreeing with him, Elaine smiled as she closed the door whispering, "I'll only be a moment. Don't start without me."

With the bar being very busy that night, it was about fifteen minutes before she returned with the bottle of wine. Joyce was already in bed, quietly waiting with the covers pulled up to her chin. Standing stark naked, wearing only his wire-rimmed glasses, she handed her client his bottle of wine. She then proceeded to the vanity where she began to disrobe. She did not look at him directly but instead gazed at his nakedness through the mirror. Her eyes ranged freely up and down his body, staring adoringly. She could not help admire his masculine figure and how he resembled the Greek god Apollo. For the first time in her career, she felt lust for the flesh, and her expectations were that this was going to be an enjoyable evening. Jokingly, while still undressing, Elaine turned and asked Joyce how good he was.

Not receiving a reply, she felt Joyce had not heard her, and she walked closer while repeating the question. She found it strange that Joyce still had not responded. Walking over to her bedside, she got an eerie feeling as she looked at her friend. Not observing any movement, it seemed unnatural the way Joyce lay there, having no reaction, except for a constant stare at the ceiling, without a slightest twitch, or blink of an eye.

It was obvious from her lifeless body that something was terribly wrong, and her worry now elevated to fear. She had not realized that Joyce was already dead and had died from a powerful twisting jerk that had snapped her neck, killing her silently and instantly.

He was behind her now as she turned, and concerned, she asked him what had happened to Joyce. Not saying a word, Elaine saw him raise his arm, holding the wine high in the air, and before she knew it, he smashed her head with the bottle, dropping her to the floor.

The room began to spin around and around as she tried her best to see through the obscurity of her blurred vision. Semiconscious, weak, and her head bleeding profusely, she feared for her life, knowing she was going to die. At that moment, she felt her body suddenly being lifted up, and he placed her on the bed next to Joyce. Regaining some senses, yet still unsteady, she could see his silhouette as he stood at the side of the bed looking down at her. Her emotions began to heighten. She did not want to die, and she wanted to cry out, plead, beg him for her life, but she was incapable of doing so. Her body felt completely numb and her fingertips were tingling. Her senses were there, but somehow her brain refused to respond in the way she wanted, and she came to realize that she had lost total control of her speech and body functions.

Again the shadow appeared. This time it hovered closely over her, and she could feel his breath upon her face. She couldn't make out exactly what he was doing, being so close to her, except for that shiny object that quickly flashed across her face. Soon the shadow moved away from the candle, and the light was once again admitted. Elaine, placing her hand to her neck, could feel the coagulation of blood, this much she was able to acknowledge. Her instinct now warned her that her end had come, and being so numb, she had not even felt the blade that had just slashed her throat.

******

After the brutal murders were committed, he began to dress. Taking his leisure time, he picked up the candle by the bed and carried it over to the vanity where he placed it across from the other. Standing between the two lit candles, he leaned over and put his face against the mirror, looking closely at his reflection. He then removed his glasses, exposing the white pupil of his eye and smiled smartly as he marveled over his slender features. He became dazzled by what he saw and could not get over the new profile Isabel had given him. With delight, he posed at different angles, turning his face side-to-side, unable to get enough of his youthful appearance. For this night was surely a night of witchery, and Dutch had enjoyed every minute of it. With the clock rolled back twenty-five years, he felt virile, and for the first time in his life, by Isabel's means, he was able to speak, a pleasure he had been deprived of his entire life.

Nevertheless, to make his mission complete, Dutch felt he had to carry out one final objective before he left. Dipping his fingers into the blood of his victim's throat, he wrote on the surface of the mirror, "reflections of an imposter." He wanted to add suspense, intrigue to his message, and give the case a new twist for the police who were already baffled by the previous murders.

The following day, Gibbs and Moore were called in to investigate the deaths of the two prostitutes. The chambermaid, early that morning, had been making her rounds changing the linens when she discovered the two women dead in bed. Shocked by the horror of it, she let out a blood-curdling scream as she ran frantically through the hall, trembling the whole way down the stairs shouting, "Murder, murder!"

The two inspectors on the scene forbid anyone from entering the room as they combed every inch, searching for possible clues. Looking at the women lying before them, a quick examination showed that Joyce's neck had been broken. As Gibbs leaned over to take a closer look at her friend, he further deduced that Elaine's death had not occurred as instantaneously as Joyce's had. With a large gash to the head and a slit throat, he concluded that her wounds had not been inflicted simultaneously. Neither woman was bound, and he felt it was feasible to assume that they had died separately and had been placed on the bed together for the killer's amusement.

On the floor next to the bed, he saw a bottle of wine. Although it was unbroken, the label appeared to have bloodstains on it, and he guessed that it was the blunt instrument used to bash Elaine's head. He visualized that whoever had committed such a crime had to be a very powerful person in order to snap a neck and cut a throat as deeply as he had.

Whether it was the killer's carelessness or his sheer intent, the knife was left behind on the table for the police to discover, and this struck Gibbs as an obvious mistake. It was neither a bowie knife nor a switchblade chosen by the killer. It was an ordinary kitchen knife, which seemed to be part of an expensive set, unaffordable to any common person.

Apparently, the killer was by no means a professional; a little sloppy, he had left far too many clues around. He had given the police his handwriting when he left his message on the mirror and exposed his intellect; he was by no means illiterate. Gazing at the mirror, Gibbs looked at the blood-written message, trying to decipher the killer's meaning. As he speculated on the message, it was not at all clear. The word reflection he quickly understood but when it came to the word imposter, he was a little bewildered by the killer's interpretation. To Gibbs, the definition of the word was plain and simple, but the killer's message could have had many meanings. Thinking on, he felt that the killer could have very well been in disguise. According to the testimony, facts, and eyewitness accounts of the people with whom Gibbs had spoken, all distinctly remembered one thing; the killer was very tall and broad. Even the waitress, who had served him, claimed he had never spoken a word when she brought them their drinks, only recalling a smile and a wink as he tossed a half a crown on her tray as a generous tip. The innkeeper also remarked that he was certainly not a local, never having set eyes on him until that night.

Not knowing anyone else who could fit the killer's description of broad size, Dutch quickly came into Inspector Gibbs' mind. Being extremely large, he felt the potential was likely. After all, he could have worn a disguise and changed his appearance where no one was able to recognize him, and according to Gibbs' intuition, this could easily account for the killer's meaning when he wrote his message on the mirror, "reflections of an imposter." Nevertheless, Gibbs felt he should bring Dutch in, just the same, for an inquiry, and in doing so, he would at least have the satisfaction of knowing one way or another.

One good thing had resulted from this saga and that was Shawn had been vindicated of the crime. Gibbs made a mental note that as soon as he returned to the jail, he would promptly release him. Isabel would be ecstatic by that decision, of that he was sure.

It was also that morning that Gibbs had received Doctor Lane's complete autopsy report for Nancy and Peggy. According to Dr. Lane's examination, there was nothing that could substantiate a murder. He was shocked by the contents of the report and the facts within. He noted that the heart had not burst and the hyoid bone was still intact which ruled out all, if any, suspicion of strangulation. Reading further with keen interest, he saw that the bodies of the victims showed no inflammation or perforation of the stomach lining or esophagus. There were also no toxins such as cyanide, strychnine, or arsenic found in the blood stream or the body that would indicate poisoning. Not one shred of evidence supported an unnatural death. In short, the autopsy report was inconclusive. Both the victims' hearts had just stopped for some unknown reason, which Doctor Lane was unable to determine.

Despite the report's findings, Gibbs had his own suspicions and was convinced the deaths were nothing less than a plot for murder. The bodies bound as they were had been in itself an admission to the facts and truth. The details he witnessed all pointed to foul play; someone had gone through great lengths to change the facts. After reading the report, he realized that someone had something to hide and had tried to cover it up. But why, he thought? Why would they go to such great lengths to make it appear to look like strangulation?

Somehow, his gut feeling sensed it was poisoning. He admitted he was baffled, not only by the evidence or lack of it, but also by Doctor Lane's report. He had been so sure the cause of death would have been discovered during the autopsy. Since the report was inconclusive on the cause of death, he was now left in the dark, posed with the problem of how they were murdered. There was nothing to substantiate their deaths, no wounds, no abrasions, not even one shred of evidence found to support his suspicions of poisoning. After all, people's hearts just don't stop at the spur of the moment, especially two people at the same time.

To arrest someone, he knew he needed proof of the crime, and this, in itself, left him with a weak case. How could he accuse a murderer of a crime without knowing the cause of death? One thing was certain; the killer had no way of knowing that the poison would be undetected. For if the killer had, he wouldn't have gone to such great lengths to cover up the facts when their deaths would have simply appeared to be from natural causes, eliminating all, if any, suspicion. He was aware that this case was not going to be an easy one. Nevertheless, he was determined to see it through to the end and unmask the murderer, solving this horrendous puzzle.

******

The following morning Isabel was sitting in her solarium waiting for Dutch to bring her breakfast. As he wheeled in the servant's table and poured a cup of tea for her, she curiously looked up at his face, closely watching his reactions. She was a little apprehensive as to whether or not he had any memory of last night's whereabouts. She was sure if he had, he would have handed her one of his little notes stating his concerns or troubles.

Not seeing anything out of the ordinary, she assumed all was well, and he did not give her any reason to feel he remembered even a single iota of the event. As it was, he was expected to return late in the evening, and during his sleep, the transformation of the spell would take place, restoring him back and erasing any recollection of his ordeal.

She was pleased the two women had met their disastrous ends. Resting easily, she was consumed with thoughts of contentment, knowing their knowledge of Shawn had been permanently silenced. All that was left was to reckon with Reverend Peterson.

At that moment, her concentration was broken as she was distracted by the disturbing sounds of the doorknocker. Whoever it was seemed quite persistent, she thought! Being a room away, she listened intently for Dutch to respond. Again the pounding continued, this time with more intensity, and Dutch still had not responded. Unable to bear the noise any longer, she shot up from the breakfast table in a huff, and annoyed, she answered the door, only to be surprised by the unexpected guest.

There, at the doorway, was Shawn smiling with Gibbs and a police escort close behind. Blissfully, her eyes brimmed with excitement, and she dashed toward him, locking in an embrace. Overcome with emotion, tears quickly filled her eyes and streamed freely down her face. So overwhelmed by her son's presence, she nearly forgot that Gibbs was a spectator to this delightful reunion. Composing herself, she apologized for her distraction and thanked the inspector for being so good as to bring her son home.

It had not occurred to her at first, but as she gazed at the police escort, she distinctively became alarmed and suspiciously questioned their motives for this visit. She was dismayed to hear that they had come to take Dutch into custody. Fitting the description of the murderer, Gibbs wanted to question Dutch under an intense interrogation in hopes of clearing up any matters of suspicion on his behalf.

Dutch, who had returned from the basement with a pail of coal, overheard Gibbs' explanation for his arrest. It was very unlikely that he would ever allow such an arrangement to happen. Having claustrophobia, the thought of being placed in a cramped cell, secluded in a four wall enclosure, would drive him mad, and he would rather have faced death than submit to imprisonment.

Not wanting to see her loyal servant dragged away, Isabel tried her best to make excuses for Dutch by claiming he was with her for a good portion of the night. Gibbs, unswayed by her testimony, insisted he had to take him in just the same to satisfy himself. With Isabel's permission, they separated and scoured each room of the house to conduct a thorough search.

Each took a different path combing the ground floor while Gibbs' search brought him into the kitchen. Pausing before the butcher's block, he took note of an empty slot in the knife rack on the side of the table. As the opportunity arose, still having the murder weapon with him in his inside jacket pocket, he removed it to carefully compare the details of the knives. There was no doubt that the knife belonged to the set, composed of fine quality steel with a grip that had a black ridge handle that was securely fastened by three brass rivets. Each knife had its own unique signature of the Wilken Blade and Company's trademark stamped on it. Enthusiastically pressing further, his optimism was now heightened by not only the discovery of the brand name, but also by how nicely it fit in the slot. His last observation was again drawn to that very knife and how its blade length fit so evenly in its rightful order of sequence, with the cleaver toward the end. It was a perfect match, and there was no doubt in his mind whatsoever that the murder weapon had come from this very place.

Just then, Isabel entered the kitchen and inquired if he had any luck locating Dutch. Nodding his head no, without being noticed he placed the murder weapon back in his pocket and twisted around to face her, replying, "I doubt we will ever find him here now."

While the rest of the party assembled in the kitchen, all unsuccessful in their searches as well, Gibbs gave Isabel a word of advice. He suggested that, for all practical matters, she convince Dutch to turn himself in, rather than be on the wanted list. He thoroughly understood Dutch's disability and promised he would give him every opportunity and benefit of a fair inquiry to clear his name. Not having anything else of importance to discuss, Gibbs departed with his party and was led out by Isabel who closed the door behind them.

At that precise moment, she realized what a precarious situation she had created for Dutch. So blinded by her anxiousness to release her son from jail, she never anticipated the backlash of her actions. Disturbed and cold, she rubbed her hands as she walked nervously into the parlor and sat in her armchair, contemplating what she was to do. She never foresaw her carelessness and she reprimanded herself. How could she ever make this up to him? He had now become a fugitive by her own making, and she was genuinely sorry. Shamefully she turned away, and just then, she noticed the pail full of coal left in front of the bookshelf. Not seeing the contents emptied out into the coal bin, she knew exactly where Dutch had gone.

Jumping quickly to her feet, she dashed out of the rear door of the manor and made a straight path to the family's crypt. If her suspicions were correct, that is where Dutch would be found. Pushing aside the large squeaky gate, she entered the crypt, walking down the few steps leading to the chamber. There she paused, looking around the room for a few seconds before she uttered a sound. She knew he was there; she could feel his presence. In a whisper she spoke out into the darkness, "They have gone away. It's safe for you to come out now."

Instantly, Dutch, who had been hiding behind a family vault, came out from the shadows and into clear view. He had trust in Isabel and did not believe she would ever betray him. Pitifully, he stood there looking at her as if he wanted to cry. This was the first time in her life she had witnessed him act in such a way, like a little boy who had lost a loved one and was heartbroken.

Sure of his innocence, he could not believe he was being accused of murder. Sad and fearful, she could see in his eyes that he was reaching out to her for help. The eyes being the windows of emotion tell it all, and as she looked at his expression, she was able to see his wants, his needs, and his despair. It was evident that he was lost and did not know what to do, and to her everlasting regret, she was so sorry, more than anyone could imagine. She admitted she had made an awful mistake and felt terrible knowing she had wronged him. Having no answers to comfort him, she only had the words of a promise she hoped to keep. Feeling his hurt, she wanted to cry as well. Weak with anxiety, she could not bear to have him know that she was the culprit that betrayed the trust.

Although it was not intentional, she still accepted accountability and criticized herself for the horrific blunder. All that she was able to do for him now was to see to his comfort and harbor him any way she could. She insisted he always use the tunnel every time he came for food and dry clothes. She would make sure the coast was clear when he was ready to enter the house. If ever she had an unexpected guest, she would leave a lit candle by the parlor window, signaling him not to come until the candle was extinguished.

At least the secret tunnel now served a purpose for Dutch's safety, and she was thankful to her great grandfather who had built it eighty-seven years ago. Prompted by his wife's death during childbirth and feeling the need to visit her on a daily basis, he was inspired to construct this unusual passageway. He dreaded the cold, disliked the high snow, and came up with the idea of making a tunnel that would connect the manor to the family crypt. With a span of two thousand feet, he had it built with a secret passageway, which led from the parlor and exited from a bogus floor vault in the crypt. For his convenience, he also had the masons construct a crypt fireplace so that he could stay warm during his visits.

After his wife's passing, he was a very lonely man. He had loved her very much. So much so, that even after her death, he wanted to be near her. Having the solitude and solace he desired, it gave him comfort to sit by her crypt and talk to her as if she was still alive, explaining all events and family matters to her. They thought he was mad the way he carried on conversations, speaking alone in the dimly lit room filled with the dead.

He never had the urge or the need to remarry and start over again, considering he was still youthful at the age of forty-seven. Love, being the mysterious emotion that it is, would explain why it extended beyond the grave. He could not wait to be reunited with his love, and that was probably why, shortly after the tunnel was built, he died from a broken heart, sitting in his chair next to her crypt.

Chapter XIV

The Forbidden Relationship

It was tragic for Rachel that her family found out about Shawn. Now common knowledge and the talk of the town, they felt betrayed by her secrecy and disobedience. While Rachel knew her family would not embrace the news of her involvement with Shawn with open arms, she never expected them to react in such a drastic way.

Her father angrily forbade her from ever seeing Shawn again. Prompted by disappointment, the family lost trust in her and no longer allowed her out of the house alone. Restricting her freedom, she was only able to leave the house when accompanied by a servant or family member. These harsh conditions created a problem for the two lovers who wanted so much to be at each other's side.

For the entire day, Shawn waited faithfully at their favorite rendezvous spot for Rachel and began to worry over her absence, especially after not receiving word from her of any change of plans. They had been inseparable, and it was very unlikely that Shawn would remain idle without finding out what had happened to his love.

Late that evening he ventured to the Thompsons' estate. Longing to be reunited with her, he planned this unexpected visit to surprise

Rachel, so they could spend time together. Having been to Rachel's estate once before, Shawn knew that her bedroom window was in line with the main gate and was able to find it without a problem. On arrival, he halted his horse parallel to the eight-foot mason wall. Standing on the saddle, he could easily reach the top, and he pulled himself up and scaled the wall, quietly making his approach to the mansion.

However, Shawn was unaware of the three mastiffs that guarded the estate grounds, keeping out all unwanted intruders. Extremely large and very aggressive, the three mastiffs, incredibly powerful and acting as a team, were quite capable of killing a full-grown lion. With this being the case, if Shawn were ever caught by the jaws of one of those creatures, he would have no chance for survival. Nevertheless, with luck on his side and as quiet as he was, the dogs, being on the far side of the estate, did not hear him approach.

Seeing Rachel's room emanating light from a lit candle, he assumed she was still awake and proceeded with caution. With a use of a tree adjacent to the structure, he climbed the massive oak to the second floor window. From where he stood, he looked in and saw his love resting comfortably in her bed reading a book. To her surprise, he tapped lightly on her windowpane, trying not to arouse any other members of the household.

With eyes beaming, she caught sight of Shawn. Excitedly, she sprung from her bed and rushed to the window to greet him with open arms, so overjoyed to see him that she smothered him with hugs and kisses. For the moment, their existing pain had subsided, and life was now rejuvenated with nothing else seeming to matter. Their world that had been torn apart was restored by the passion of their love.

Shawn entered into the room where they again embraced and kissed excessively, making their way slowly toward the bed. Rachel was happy that he had come and found this moment to be a perfect opportunity to break some news to him.

Taking both his hands into hers, closely watching his reaction, she gazed into his eyes and announced she was with child and he was to be a father. Underestimating him, she did not expect him to react as he did. She somehow felt he would be a little disheartened by the news, considering the timing was not right with all the troubles they had to face, having two families who were bitter rivals and a relationship that was now in turmoil.

To her astonishment, he instead was overjoyed by her revelation and felt perhaps he should approach her father and ask for her hand in marriage. However, Rachel knew that was a bad idea. She also knew well that her father and brothers would not take kindly to this, and knowing their crazed behavior, she feared they would probably kill him on the spot.

Rachel insisted on his silence, explaining that she would rather break the news to her mother first. She felt if anyone would understand, it would be her mother. She was much more rational and level headed and could cope with matters such as these, taking the unwelcome news far better than her father would. She hoped her mother would see things her way and hoped to use her as a go-between who could settle the differences within the family. She was worried this would not go over very well and feared for Shawn, prompting severe harm against him.

Around two in the morning, Rachel's father, enjoying a late snack, made his usual venture into the kitchen where he would help himself to a piece of bread and a slice of cured ham. This early morning craving drew his suspicions as he passed his daughter's room. Always finding her lights out at this particular hour of the night, he became aroused as he saw the light glowing from underneath the crack of the door. Being curious, he paused for a moment, putting his ear flush to the door and then quickly opening it. The sight outraged him as he found the two intimate lovers lying in bed.

Uncontrollably he lunged for Shawn, his voice ascending to a murderous falsetto, but Rachel's quick thinking prevented an assault as she jumped up and tossed the blanket over her father's head, pulling him down to the floor. Her father pinned down with her body weight gave Shawn the advantage to quickly dress and escape. With only his pants and boots on, he desperately made a dash for the window, dropping his laced shirt in the process. While making his climb down the tree, Rachel's father managed to break free and shouted loudly out the window, unsettling the peacefulness of the night.

The mastiffs that had been resting now heard the ruckus and dashed off into the direction of the disturbance. Finishing the last few feet of his descent, Shawn heard the dogs not far off and approaching in a mad frenzy. He realized time was crucial and he had to reach the wall before the dogs were upon him or suffer a vicious attack. Running with all his might, he did not remember the wall being that far away. It seemed endless this time as he ran for his life with the intensity of the dogs' approach closing the gap.

Terrorized, he had a quick change of mind. He decided against jumping up the eight-foot wall, worried that he might not make the leap to freedom and instead headed for the main entrance, feeling he had a better chance of safely scaling the bar gate. The dogs were just yards behind him when Shawn made his leap onto the gate. Dreyfus, the most vicious of the three, happened to grab his right foot with his powerful jaws and began to apply crushing pressure to his ankle. Enduring excruciating pain, he was in a desperate fight for survival as the mighty mastiff pulled on him with such jerking force. Back and forth the tug of war continued, and with the pain becoming unbearable, he realized he could not keep up the struggle for much longer. It was unbelievable, he thought, the overwhelming power that this creature had and how the dog used its body weight to try to pull him down. Panic began to set in as he felt his hands begin to sweat and lose their grip. If the dog bore down just one more time, he was sure he would lose his grip and fall to his death. Having no choice, he gave one more try to break free, and pulling with all his might, his foot slipped out of the boot, saving him from a doomed fate.

At six in the morning, Rachel's sleep was disturbed by the sounds of sawing and chopping. Rising from her bed, she tiredly strolled across her room toward her window to see what was causing all the commotion. Gazing through the panes of her closed window, she saw the servants hard at work cutting down the tree under the supervision of her father. As he looked up with sharpened eyes and flushed face, she quickly drew the curtains closed once eye contact was made. She knew from his stern look that he was furious as well as hurt. That oak tree had meant so much to him. As a lad of seven, he and his grandfather had planted it, and therefore, it had much sentimental value for him. It must have devastated him to destroy it, for that would account for the rash measures he was taking, apparently weighing his pride over his passion.

Unfortunately, this day of anguish was far from over. That very afternoon Rachel's father and two brothers visited the Laughton Estate, wanting to have a word with Isabel.

He was a high-strung, vulgar man who was very demanding and had to have things go his way. Rather than conducting his affairs in a civilized manner, which would have been the appropriate way of presenting himself, he was far from diplomatic. Gruff and to the point, he was not at all charming, and after many years of bad example, it was easy to see why his sons were no different.

Pounding forcefully on the front door, Isabel opened it quickly to find out what was causing the awful racket. Looking down at Rachel's father with a scorching look, she wondered what prompted him to hit the door so vigorously with the heel of a boot. Not realizing she was Isabel, he assumed she was just one of the servants since she was wearing an apron and holding a feather duster. Agitated and wearing a stony expression, he demanded, "I wish to speak with the master of the house. I have a matter of grave importance to discuss, so please don't try my patience. Fetch her at once."

Led into the parlor, he and his sons were invited to make themselves comfortable while Isabel excused herself for a moment. It was not more than a minute before the squabbling began between the two brothers, both hotheaded, bickering in a heated debate as to what manner of procedure they should undertake. Upon her entry, standing silently at the door, Isabel remained there observing the dispute. Undignified and not at all acting like gentlemen, it became evident from their mannerisms that they were of poor grace and lacked social finesse. Not realizing she had been a spectator to their bitter exchange, their embarrassment was soon met by silence once her presence became noted. From the corner of the room, the oldest brother, who was the boldest, turned forward and began to express his discontent with Shawn when Isabel cut him short, stating she would not hear from him and would only speak to his father.

From the background, Isabel could hear his grumbling as he rose from the chair bellowing out, "Very well, Madam." Nearsighted, he walked over to Isabel. He became a bit surprised once his vision cleared and he saw that the servant he had earlier encountered was indeed Isabel.

"Forgive my ill manner, Madam, for mistaking you for the servant of the house. I had no way of knowing. You had me at a disadvantage."

"I doubt very much that would have made a difference toward your behavior. What is it that is so urgent that you practically tore down my door?"

With sharpened eyes and a pitched voice, he began, "Do you see what I hold in my hand? A boot and a laced shirt! And do you know where I obtained them and to whom they belong?"

Not wishing to give him any satisfaction, she stated, "No, but I'm sure you are going to tell me," rolling her eyes and exhaling in disgust.

"They belong to your son! I was outraged by his immoral behavior as he violated my daughter right under my roof. His sheer presence ran my blood feverish as I felt a murderous streak come over me, catching him in the blasphemous act of seducing my daughter with woos of impurity in her bedchamber."

"You mean your daughter and my son had consensual sex in your house?" she taunted.

"Please, the word offends me and so does your son. I cannot believe for an instant that it was consensual. Your filthy son forced himself upon my daughter."

With eyes blazing, she spoke in a rugged burst, "Filthy son? If you are going to pass judgment, I suggest you begin with the likes of your two screeching gutter rats whom I witnessed earlier, bickering and fighting in my parlor."

"Forget the boys!" he shouted, raising his temperament to a flushed face. "You missed the point, Madam. My daughter's no longer a virgin. She's been violated."

"I'm sorry to have to be the one to inform you but your daughter lost her virginity a long time ago. Their affair's been going on behind your back for quite some time. I assure you, it was consensual. They're in love. Apparently, you have not noticed."

"Love my ass! I will not hear of it. Your son's conduct was shameful and his morals indecent. He was only after one thing, and apparently, he got his way. I assure you, he will not see my Rachel anymore. I give fair warning. If I ever catch your son with my daughter again, I will not hesitate to shoot. Do I make myself clear, Madam?"

Not saying a word to the accusations, Isabel gave him not the least satisfaction nor a bit of sympathy as she stood there with a vacuous expression. Instead, she was uninterested in his convictions toward her son, relaying her feelings bluntly, "If that's all you have to say, then I assume you will be leaving."

He had at least expected some sort of apology. Feeling resentment and a lack of any cooperation, he knew by her contemptuous remarks that she intentionally wished to be offensive and humiliate him before his sons. Not willing to endure any more of her disrespectful insults, he withdrew from her home in a huff, feeling much angrier than he had when he arrived.

After their departure, she gave the circumstances rational thought. She realized that there was a difference between a daughter and a son, and therefore, she could not blame him for his outrage in the matter. After all, as a parent, his concerns were for his daughter's welfare, and he wanted to see her follow in the respectful traditions of matrimony.

But the one thing that worried Isabel the most was the threat he promised to carry out. This gravely concerned her for she knew he had meant it, and she felt the need to do something to prevent it from ever happening. Normally, she would have taken harsh measures against Rachel's father. Since his principles in this situation were justified, she decided a disablement would better suit her purposes to ward off any threats that he might impose on Shawn.

That very evening while Isabel was having dinner with her son, the events of the day weighed heavily on her mind. She had much to discuss with him, having certain things she wanted to clarify. She felt this was a good time as any to confront him and understand exactly how he felt for Rachel and where their relationship was going.

Despite the many obstacles that lay before them and the recent tragedy, she wanted to be a part of his life and help in any way she could. She was concerned about his happiness, even though the future looked grim and troublesome and his relationship with Rachel now seemed very uncertain. Naturally, she did not want to see any harm come to him and had to warn him of the threats made by Rachel's father. With their relationship now treacherous, she rationalized it might not be worth the risk if love was not truly there.

Confronting Shawn, she questioned him on the extent of his love for Rachel. At first, he was reluctant to discuss his affairs, but feeling as he did for his mother, he gave into her qualms just to satisfy her. Not concealing a thing, he explained it all, from his secret rendezvous, his most recent encounter with Rachel's father, and his narrow escape from death by the jaws of Dreyfus. It was an earful for Isabel, and she was overwhelmed by the events, especially the close brush he had with death.

She thought she had heard it all when suddenly he announced that Rachel was pregnant with his child. Filling her glass with wine, she felt weak from the unexpected news and had to sit down. At that precise moment, she could feel the blood rush to her head. She was well aware that this would enflame an already intense, complex situation. She was sure that once the news reached Rachel's father, there would be no stopping him and feared he would come after Shawn, fulfilling his threat. She was sorry she had asked, having underestimated the intensity of the affair.

After dinner, drained from the excitement, she retired to the parlor where she sat in front of the fireplace. Shawn, knowing his mother felt extremely cold when she was nervous, built a fire for her. Noting her sheer silence, he saw she wanted to be left alone. Passing the time, she became mesmerized, watching the flames dance before her face. Engrossed in her disconcerting thoughts, she tried to imagine what to do with Rachel's father.

Suddenly, she was startled by a noise of a latch and a squeak from a hinge that emanated from the corner of the darkened room. She could feel the chill of a cold breeze radiate out as Dutch made his exit from the tunnel's passageway. Although Isabel had not expected him to arrive so soon, she had been prepared, keeping his food warm in a cast iron pot before the fireplace. With a warm smile, she asked how he was feeling. Nodding his head, she assumed his answer to be well and realized he was a bit hungry as he headed straight for the pot, placing his nose over the mouth-watering stew.

Bent down on one knee, she noticed that he was also cold as he extended his hands and rubbed them together by the open fire. It was then, as she observed Dutch, that she was struck with the most brilliant idea, giving her the solution to deal with Rachel's father, which she so desperately sought.

******

The following morning Rachel's mother woke to cries of agonizing pain. Frightened out of her wits, she jumped from her bed as her husband carried on like a mad man. She had no concept of what was ailing him and tried to get his attention by repeatedly asking what was wrong. Not responding, he tossed the blankets off himself as he rose from the bed looking at the disfigurement of his hands. With his eyes wide and bulging, he was engulfed with disbelief as he tried to understand what exactly was happening to him. Ridden by shock, he was unable to take his eyes off his hands as he stretched out his arms and looked at his crippled, deformed fingers.

He tried his best to make sense of this strange phenomenon, feeling the stiffness of his joints accompanied by painful inflammation and swelling. He realized the deformity he was suffering had to be related to some sort of severe rheumatism. He was aware that there were diabolical forces that were beyond his grasp. Not having any logical explanation as to why he was suddenly stricken with this ailment, all that was left was the firm belief that he must have been bewitched.

Chapter XV

The Agony of Apprehension

For some time Gibbs had his suspicions about Isabel and felt she was not at all truthful about her involvement in harboring Dutch. He had his doubts about Dutch, not believing he was accustomed enough with the woods to be able to independently survive off the land. He knew, in order for him to keep up his existence, he had to seek refuge some place with which he was familiar and be helped by someone he trusted.

Secretly, Inspector Gibbs had Isabel's home and property under surveillance prior to Dutch's arrest and had been watching the estate around the clock. With only two police officers on the force and Dutch being such a large man, Gibbs decided he needed the assistance of temporary recruits, feeling there would be much resistance upon his apprehension. Through the course of their observations, they had recently discovered that Dutch had been using the family's crypt for some time as his hideaway. Watching his pattern, they had also learned, while peeking through a small hole in a stained glass window, that Dutch had access to a secret tunnel that led to Isabel's home. This, of course, would account for why he had never been seen making his rounds in and out of the manor and why he was so well provided for with daily supplies of food, fresh clothes, and plenty of candles. After observing him long enough, a plan was devised to move in and capture him while he rested during his afternoon nap.

With the plan set in motion, the first phase was for a group of five to storm into the crypt and overpower Dutch as he slept, while the remaining parties positioned themselves just outside as backup, preventing any escape from the perpetrator. However, the tactical group who was to start the assault was unaware that the squeaky gate would announce their presence.

Dutch, awakened by the metallic sound, stood ready by the door as the five men charged in toward him. Overwhelmingly, he swept through the party of men as easily as paper tossed by a violent wind. With one blow of his powerful fist he broke the collarbone of his first attacker, while the two who followed close behind in pursuit were tossed to the side like rag dolls, hitting hard against the stone vaults. As the fourth man approached, he was taken by surprise as he was lifted completely off his feet in a bear hug and slammed unconscious against the mason wall. The fifth man, flabbergasted by the sight, stopped dead in his tracks, ridden by fear. Never witnessing such a display of strength unleashed by one man, he turned and called to his comrades for more backup.

With a rush of the remaining party scrambling into the crypt, Dutch, cornered in front of the chapel, knew he was now trapped and had nowhere to turn to make an escape. Desperately, he mustered all his strength and dislodged a four-foot marble statue from its base. Taking a deep breath, he lifted the huge stone figure above his head and turned with the bulky weight to face his pursuers. Coming to a complete halt, they were instinctively warned to dare not take another step. Holding the statue before them, all he needed to do was toss it out, and several of them would be crushed to death. Held by that threat, they were kept at bay, frozen, too afraid to move an inch. They knew he was physically powerful, but they had never anticipated the magnitude of his strength until the struggle began.

Suddenly, he took a second breath and with that, he stepped toward them as they quickly moved out of harm's way. He did not intend to injure them. He just wanted to get away. Making a brave attempt, he smashed the statue through the stained glass window, creating a large enough gap to make his escape through the rear.

Familiar with the terrain, he headed for the high ground where the woods were deep and heavily populated. Running for some time, he could hear the hounds on his trail, not far off and in hot pursuit. Reaching the plateau, he came to a halt, unable to run any further. He was devastated as he realized he had miscalculated his escape and had cornered himself at the edge of a cliff with a waterfall before him.

He attempted to backtrack, but it was too late. The party was already upon him. Desperately, he considered his options, gazing over the cliff's edge. Although there were jagged rocks at the bottom and a jump that was too high, his main concern was the simple fact that he could not swim. He was determined not to be taken by the police. Claustrophobic, he would rather face death than be placed in a cramped cell, driven to madness. Having no other alternative, he knew he had to make a stand. As the party began to close in around him, he stood firm and ready, turning a cold eye on his pursuers.

Not wanting to see blood shed, Gibbs approached Dutch alone and tried to talk him into giving himself up peacefully. Seeing he was not willing to surrender so easily, three large volunteers mistakenly took the initiative to make their move.

With a bitter exchange, Dutch quickly knocked each of the two men to the ground with single blows while the third remained in a clench. Desperately needing assistance, Inspector Gibbs' call for aid was met by four more men who intervened and intensified the confrontation further. Unrelentingly, Dutch fought on as five men tried their best to wrestle him to the ground. He refused to be captured and give in to the fight. He saw the conflict was coming to an end as more men moved in to join the skirmish. Standing close to the cliff's edge, he knew there was no other choice as he gazed down, making his final decision over his fate. With all his might, he leaped out and plunged to his death, taking along two unfortunate souls.

******

That evening Isabel became concerned when Dutch still had not arrived for his evening meal. Well past his expected hour, she began to wonder what could be detaining him so long. With nightfall upon them and the evening brisk, Dutch would have been in front of the fireplace by now in the comfort of a warm house enjoying a hearty meal. He was like clockwork, always on time, faithfully arriving between the hours of seven and eight in the evening after making his exit from the tunnel. But tonight his arrival seemed to be a bit off schedule, and she felt uneasy, afraid that something might be wrong.

Parting the curtains to one side, she gazed out the window repeatedly, eager to catch a glimpse of him. Waiting up for most of the night, it was past two in the morning when fatigue set in and she decided to retire to her bedchamber.

Optimistically, she gave Dutch the benefit of the doubt and assumed all was well, hoping he would show up later. As she left the parlor, her thoughts were with him, and she tossed a few extra logs onto the fire to keep the crock warm, so when he did arrive, he would have a hot meal to eat.

As quick as she closed her eyes to sleep was as quick as she rose that following morning, the night flowing by like a flash. Rising from her bed in haste, she freshened up and raced down the stairs, quickly heading in a straight path for the parlor. She was concerned whether Dutch had arrived and had eaten his meal during the night.

Disappointed, she saw the crock was untouched, and she seriously began to worry. Before she could think on the subject, a hard knock sounded at the front door, announcing a presence. She could tell by the rapid pounding that it must be important. Responding to the caller, she quickly opened the door to find Inspector Gibbs with a carriage and driver behind him. His grim expression was a warning of the grievous news she was about to receive. Expressing his condolences, he explained the ordeal leading to Dutch's death.

Having no known relatives, Gibbs needed someone to identify the body for the record and felt she was the appropriate choice since she

105

had known Dutch so well. Although she was devastated by the news, she agreed to do so and immediately accompanied Gibbs back to town. As she walked into the mortuary, she felt a chill run down her spine as she entered into a room that had a single cadaver, which she assumed to be Dutch.

Slowly approaching the corpse, she was distraught as Gibbs lifted the sheet, uncovering the face. Once placing her eyes on him, she immediately felt faint and her face turned chalk white, desperately needing to sit. Overcome with distress, she placed her hand to her forehead, sobbing his loss. The memory of his tragedy would be imbedded in her mind forever. Haunted by that image, she realized that her actions had driven him to this fate. If only he were alive, she would tell him how sorry she truly was for her actions and explain the whole truth that he deserved to know.

She did not care about herself or her reputation any longer. What really mattered to her was to correct her wrong and free herself of the regrettable pain with which she now had to live. Wanting the best for Dutch, she would spare no expense and relayed her sentiments to Gibbs. She felt he deserved a proper burial and saw no other way except to place him in her family crypt for his final resting place. Unable to bear any more of these depressing surroundings, Isabel, filled with grief, asked Gibbs if she could leave. Feeling he had imposed enough hardship upon her as it was, he agreed she could, and thanking her once again, he arranged an escort to see her safely home.

Completely exhausted, Gibbs had not had proper sleep for thirty-six hours, being on a constant move. Never in his entire career had he been as busy as he had been today, from the start of Dutch's apprehension, to the recovery of the bodies that had fallen off the cliff, and lastly his calling on Isabel. His day was far from over with many activities still needing his prompt attention. Despite being overwhelmed, he had one more engagement to keep that evening and that was with the Reverend Peterson.

It seemed that lately the reverend had a change of heart. With all the deaths that had occurred, especially those of Nancy and Peggy, he felt he could no longer remain silent, his conscience recently troubling him.

Because of their deaths, he felt the urgent need to explain the truth and reveal to Gibbs how Isabel had obtained Shawn and who was the real mother. He felt this information, and the contemptuous tension they felt for one another, might have some significance. Whether or not it had any bearing on the case, it still made him feel relieved to know the burden of the truth had been exposed.

******

After thanking the reverend for his concern, Gibbs left and returned straight to his bedside. He admitted he had a long day and was extremely tired. Fully dressed, he lay in his bed and closed his eyes, his body wanting so much to sleep. Unfortunately, his mind was not that accommodating, and subjected with the new information revealed to him, he was unable to sleep a wink thinking of his recent conversation with Reverend Peterson.

He had at least found out who was Shawn's real mother. With this new revelation, he realized that Isabel's story might have been a pretext in her apparent wish to cover up the real reason for Nancy and Peggy's visit. Understanding the circumstances that surrounded the trio, he concluded that either Isabel was in a struggle for custody, or she might have been blackmailed for money in exchange for their silence. This latest news offered a feasible explanation as to why Nancy possessed the medal on the day she died. It was conceivable that once she discovered the inscription on the medal *To Shawn, Love, Your Mother*, she might have become outraged and jealous. Not wanting Shawn to receive such a gift, she was prompted to steal it and deny him the token of Isabel's love. After all, it wasn't long after that their bodies were found.

Although the case reeked of foul play, what really baffled him the most was the substance used on the victims and his inability to identify it or establish a link between the occurrence and the crime scene. Still unable to prove his theory that poisoning was the factoring cause, he began to speculate on various theories. He did know of one substance that could have been used without detection and that was opium. Once entered into the digestive tract, it was absorbed instantly into the blood stream, quickly shut down the nervous system, stopped breathing, and the victim died shortly after. If the body was not found in the early stages of death, the opium would have dissolved into the body and not shown any traces of its toxins under the autopsy's examination. It was the perfect poisoning for the nineteen century, and his scenario looked grim, leaving him virtually without a lead.

Possibly, prior to their departure, Dutch might have taken them into captivity and injected the poison into their systems. Although it was only conjecture, he still felt he had caught his murderer, believing strongly that Dutch had committed the crimes and had then dumped Nancy's and Peggy's bodies into the river. He could not for a moment believe Isabel's complicity in the murders or that she would even sanction such a gruesome crime. He understood the complexities associated with a murderer's emotions and their influence on behavior to an abnormal degree. He was certain Dutch had acted alone and taken the responsibility on Isabel's behalf, feeling he was helping her out of an awkward situation.

Apparently, someone tall and broad had murdered the two prostitutes, and Dutch did fit the description. The evidence pointed to Dutch and he felt he had his killer. Nonetheless, the one clue that established solid proof and convinced him beyond a reasonable doubt was the knife used in the crime, which he believed to have been taken from Isabel's kitchen.

However, he needed to talk to Isabel and confront her with the truth. He hoped with the knowledge obtained he would uncover leads beneficial to the case and shed light on some unanswered questions.

Chapter XVI

A Testimony of Truth

With the case soon to be resolved, Gibbs had to leave for London on urgent business, and while there, he would inform his superiors on the progress of the investigation. During that short period, he entrusted Inspector Moore with the simple task of questioning Isabel to find out more circumstances relating to Shawn and his abandonment by his true mother.

Moore, whose mannerisms were of a repulsive, intellectual snob, may not have been the wisest choice, and his involvement would probably achieve more harm than good for the outcome of the investigation. Shawn already hated Moore since the day of his arrest and remembered well the mistreatment he received at his hands as Moore repeatedly slapped him across the face while trying to obtain his confession.

Unfortunately on the day of Moore's calling, Isabel was not at home and Shawn answered the door, greeting him with noticeable displeasure. From the very moment he confronted Moore, an atmosphere of hostility could be felt between the two. The animosity was apparent as Shawn questioned with repugnance the reason for the visit.

Inspector Moore claimed he had acquired information that needed to be verified by Shawn's mother and which could easily be settled with a few questions. Once discovering Isabel was not at home and would not be returning until the afternoon, Moore, rather than postpone the inquiry for another time, instead preferred to continue. Although the subject was sensitive, he chose to confront Shawn with the awful truth, using spitefulness over decent morals, not willing to spare him the bitter grief over his roots. Harsh and vindictive, he intentionally wished to inflict hardship by exposing the whole incident and sorrowful truth of who his real mother was.

Ridden with satisfaction, Moore saw an instant change on Shawn's face the moment of his announcement. The eyes being the window to a person's emotions, he was able to tell by their expression how much hurt he had just produced. Blinking with incredulity, he no longer wore that stern glare with a tightly clenched mouth. It was now replaced by a look of considerable despair, wounded by the breaking of the news. Provoked, he felt revulsion toward Moore. Refusing to believe it, he defensively shouted, "Lies! Nothing but lies!"

Upset and unable to bear the sinister smirk across Moore's face, Shawn sorrowfully turned away, closing the door behind him. Resting his back against the door, he was devastated and confused by the information and did not know exactly what to think. He knew Moore disliked him and felt it might be possible that he wanted to torment him where he was most vulnerable. He could not understand why he would make such a drastic accusation toward his mother, unless the allegations did have a ring of truth to them. Despite the circumstances, he did know how much he loved his mother and how very much his mother loved him and that was one thing Moore could not destroy, no matter what he said.

******

Gone for most of the morning gathering mushrooms and leeks throughout the countryside, Isabel had taken on the responsibility and predominant roles of butler, maid, and cook after Dutch had died.

She was in good spirits this evening and wanted to surprise Shawn by preparing one of his favorite meals of wild leek soup with a mixture of mushrooms and potatoes. At least this evening would certainly prove to be a testament of the love and affection that they shared for one another. Setting the table for two, wanting to make this evening a memorable one, she added a bit of elegance with the special touch of two lit candelabras and for his craving, a steaming casserole with the strong scent of leek soup.

Happily sitting at the head of the table, waiting patiently for Shawn, she was sure that once he entered the room his first instinct would be to comment on the enticing scent of his favorite meal. Not having had that particular soup for some time, his reaction would be one of pure pleasure, and she wanted to catch his initial expression to her heartfelt surprise.

Unfortunately, it was quite the contrary. When Shawn made his entrance into the dining room, looking depressed and somber, he walked over to the table and took his place at the opposite end without uttering a word. He seemed dejected; it was unusual to see him act this way. He was always bright-eyed, making a lively entrance with something to discuss about his day. Not a single comment made about the soup, and her suspicions were confirmed when she lifted the lid of the casserole and filled his dish, its delicious fragrance emanating through the air. It was evident that something was deeply disturbing him since the appetizing aroma of his favorite meal went completely unnoticed.

Quietly returning to her place, she smiled softly as she paused for a moment, hoping he would soon explain his troubled mind. Not receiving the expected reply, she took measures of her own and induced the conversation, asking him if there was something bothering him that he wanted to discuss. Seeing a tear stream down his cheek, she grew worried and rushed to his side, comforting him with a gentle touch of her hand as she caressed his face.

She was disturbed to see him unhappy and wanted to find out what was making him feel so depressed. Inquiring further, she asked once again, but this time she took his hand and held it up against her heart, nervously uttering, "Please tell me what's the matter. You are frightening me."

Avoiding eye contact, he kept his head down, not wanting her to see his face. He did not want her to notice the tears that began to flow all over again. With a sniffle and water filled eyes, he pitifully looked up at her with the want and need to embrace her and hold her tightly in his arms, assuring her of his unconditional love. She was moved by the sentiment and had no concept of what had prompted this sudden mood swing. All she did know was that he was troubled, and she wanted to find the underlying cause of this emotion. Pressing the issue, she begged him repeatedly to please tell her. Finally giving in to her pleas, she was appalled and totally unprepared for what he had to say.

Elaborating on the events of his day, Shawn began with Moore's visit and the remarkable account told to him of a baby boy abandoned by his mother and left on the doorstep of this residence.

"Apparently, Reverend Peterson made various allegations which raised questions that prompted the inspector to verify their truth. He came here today to ask you about a baby that had been left on a doorstep and if indeed, I had been that child. He somehow assumed I knew the truth of the abandonment, but once he saw my surprised reaction, he instantly realized that I had not been told at all. Although I'm not sure I believe him, he did express his regrets that he was the one to inform me of this dreadful news. He went on to say that it was vitally important that he speak with you and asked that you stop by the station to continue the discussion."

Shawn, being so distraught by the insinuation, did not need to ask but could see from his mother's eyes her culpability in the incident. He ended his story by proclaiming his love for her, noting he would always love her no matter what and that he wanted no other mother except her.

At that precise moment, she felt a rush of heat to her face. Taken by surprise, she realized the truth had been revealed. Perhaps to avoid controversy she should have prepared him for this a long time ago. Frightened as she was, she dreaded losing him, and for that reason alone, she had chosen not to divulge the truth earlier, feeling if she kept her secret safe and intact, no one could rob her of her ultimate dream.

She knew she had been wrong and selfish by what she had done, and the truth she wanted so desperately to conceal, now had come back to haunt her. She had intended to tell Shawn, but she wanted to do it on her own terms and in her own way.

Seeing the sadness within his eyes, she could tell he was heavily disheartened, and she embraced him, being there as always, providing a mother's affection. With a kiss to his forehead, she held him closely and expressed her grief by continually repeating her sorrowful regrets.

At that instant, she felt compelled to explain the truth to him, but after looking into his eyes and seeing his suffering, she decided against it, not wanting to deepen his hurt. Apparently, the timing was not right, and she felt it best to postpone the truth for a later date when he would be better prepared to receive it. Wounded deeply, he departed the dining room, needing seclusion.

She did not object nor say a word as he left the room, feeling that perhaps it was best for him to be alone, so he could contemplate on his troubles. With this pleasurable dinner turned into turmoil, she had no one to blame for this disaster except Inspector Moore.

Surrounded by solitude and ridden by guilt, she was left with nothing except the contents of her thoughts. The more she reflected, the more angry she grew. She was appalled by Moore's cunningness and how he had overstepped his bounds. Since the subject was both personal and sensitive, he should have been more discreet and only directed his discussions to her. She considered his behavior today to be unforgivable, not to mention the unforgettable treatment he had shown her son the day of his arrest. His devious actions, compounded by the brutality he had shown her son earlier, gave her more reason to hold a grudge against him.

She also had the good Reverend Peterson to thank for this revelation. If it had not been for his interfering by notifying the authorities, Moore would not have been there meddling in her business. She felt he too was accountable.

Her blood boiling, her temperament flared to a furious rage. She had never felt the instinct to kill more than she did now. Too much was happening too quickly. Still mourning the death of Dutch and the possibility of losing her son, she felt threatened by society and had a compulsion to defend all that she held dear. No one was going to take her son away from her. She vowed revenge and promised that they would be dealt with swiftly, making them all pay for their horrendous deeds.

Chapter XVII

The Deception and Tragedies

As intended, Rachel informed her mother first, feeling she would act as the peacemaker to smooth out the crisis now facing her family. Knowing her daughter so well, she had somehow suspected that something was wrong and hoped in time, her trouble would be revealed. Her daughter was a person who wore her feelings, and it was obvious by just a single glance at her expression that she had been concealing a heavy burden. Although she was not pleased with her daughter's conception, being the loving, passionate, and understanding person that she was, she did promise to help her and try to do all she could to ease the tension.

Even though she tried her best, the news was not well received by the father, and the bickering that was expected did indeed escalate as Rachel had anticipated. Although she did all she could to calm him, he still hit the roof, bursting into an uncontrollable rage. Not only had Shawn violated his daughter, he also had impregnated her, and this was totally unacceptable in his eyes.

He could think of nothing else at that moment except his urge to kill Shawn. Rushing for his gun, he made feeble attempt after attempt to load his rifle. Stricken by his handicap, suffering excruciating pain, he found himself so helpless that he shed tears of disappointment in his failure.

His decrepit fingers, swollen and twisted at the joints, made him incapable of even holding a spoon, forcing him to be fed by his wife. He knew he was a broken man both bodily and spiritually, and there was not very much he could do to personally avenge the family.

Unfortunately, the vendetta did not end there. There were still Rachel's two brothers. Being young and crazed and seeing their father's suffering, they felt the responsibility now lay with them, vowing vengeance to uphold the family's honor. Not wanting to kill Shawn outright for fear that their sister would turn them into the law, the brothers instead conspired a plan where, when the time was right, they would make his death seem like an accident.

Shrewdly, they allowed their sister to once again be reunited with Shawn. During that period, she was happy and content and felt she was able to confide in them, thinking that they had finally accepted Shawn into the family. Rachel, being trustworthy, placed her faith in them, unknowing of their sinister plan to liquidate the one she loved. Taking a different tactic, they pretended to take her side against the father, but little did she know that it was all a prearranged plot to ensnare Shawn.

On the eve of the plotted day, two weeks before Christmas, people, feeling the joys of the season, began to plan for the holidays and filled the woods in search of that one special tree to bring home and decorate. It was also a time to prepare and obtain provisions, and hunters would rush into the forest seeking their most popular prey of wild boar whose smoked hams and cured bacons would prove to be appetizing delights for the Christmas celebration.

Rachel, in high spirits since she and Shawn were together, wanted to make this Christmas a special one. She explained to her brothers that she would be gone for most of the day and would be on Shawn's property where together they would be looking for trees for both families.

Her brothers, with other intentions in mind, inconspicuously trailed her every step of the way. They were clever, hiding well from sight, and she did not have the slightest indication that she was being followed.

With an abundance of trees from which to select, they certainly had their work cut out for them. Having never enjoyed a fun filled time such as this, the two slowly browsed the woods, being fussy and particular in their selection. Finding some trees too small and skimpy, while others were too high and wide, they soon agreed on two trees, which had the most perfect size and shape.

While Shawn was busily chopping away at the eight-foot Douglas fir, Rachel, enchanted by the beauty of the countryside, admired the pine trees that were draped in snow. Flurrying lightly, she extended her palms to catch the flakes as they gently fell into her hands. She was excited and took in the pleasures of life. It was a world of splendor, and she was captivated by this winter wonderland.

Scanning the horizon, admiring the patches of woods, she turned briefly to gaze behind her and was taken by an unsuspected surprise. There, not far off, both her brothers could be seen, hiding behind a boulder with a rifle pointed at Shawn's back.

At that instant, she was struck by their deceitfulness and realized how she had misconstrued their true intentions. Out of panic, she raced to prevent Shawn from being killed. She felt that if she placed her body in the line of fire, they would not shoot with her in their sights. Unfortunately, to her dismay, her reasoning did not turn out as planned. As she raced over with her arms held high shouting, "No, no, no!" the gun discharged in the rush of the excitement, and she was hit square in the chest, falling flat on her back.

Once the brothers realized their critical error, they frantically fled the scene. With the firing of bullets heard throughout the countryside that day, Shawn just assumed a hunter had fired another shot. A hundred feet away from Rachel, he was unaware of what had just taken place. Turning briefly to see where Rachel was, he was shocked as he saw her stretched out on her back, lying in a pool of blood. Having no concept of what had happened, his only concern was to rush to her side to quickly aid her.

Seeing so much blood, he almost passed out from the disturbing sight. He realized he could not afford to faint since he needed to be strong and keep his head in order to help her. Excitedly, he tried his best to stop the bleeding. Tearing a piece of his shirt, he pressed it against the wound, hoping to slow the flow of blood. Observing her face, he took note that her rosy complexion had faded to chalk white within a blink of an eye. It happened so fast, and he contributed the change to be from rapid blood loss. He began to panic when he saw he could not slow the bleeding. With the piece of shirt already thoroughly soaked, he ripped another piece and again applied it to the wound, adding more pressure. His mind concentrated only on one thing, the blood; there was so much of it, and his urgent priority was to stop it.

Distraught, he realized that there was not very much he could do; she was going to die. He felt in the depths of his soul that he could not avoid the inevitable. At first he shouted out for help, his voice echoing through the dense woods, but not a soul heard his pleas. In sheer desperation, he looked up at the heavens, crying out in his anguish, asking God to have mercy, and sobbing thereafter. He would do anything just to see her and the baby live, even if it meant he had to give up his own life. His vision became blurred from crying, and he held her hand, looking down at her, pitifully caressing her face with a gentle touch.

The flurries that were earlier seen had now picked up with the intensity of a moderate snowfall, and he could feel the nip in the wind. As she began to shiver, he embraced her closely, trying to shield her from the bitter cold by wrapping his cloak around her slender body. Gazing upon her, he became disheartened as he saw her eyes fill and the tears that ran down her face were the tears of her sorrow.

Struggling for life, she was not willing to let go because all that she loved was before her. Affectionately, he had to kiss her just one more time, and with eyes brimming, she tried to reciprocate with a little smile. In her weakness, she made an effort to speak, but as she tried, he could see she had difficulty getting the words out. Determined, she tried again but to no avail. Her mouth quivering, it seemed she had something to say. Whatever it was, she was unable to convey her message, and he held her hand, begging her not to exert herself. Twitching from a spasm, she squeezed his hand, wanting to get his attention. She knew the moment was near, and she fought to express her love for him. Although she was unable to speak, it was important for her to have her say. With her final breath, unable to do more, she mouthed the words, "I love you."

****

It was indecent of the Thompsons to place the burden of blame for their daughter's death upon Shawn. Wanting so much to be at her wake, the family, as always, held it against him and damned the day that they had met, forbidding him from attending the funeral. They felt he had much to account for and that if it had not been for his indiscretion, Rachel would have been alive today. Now that she had passed away, the family saw no further need for his association, feeling sure contempt and wanting to be rid of him once and for all.

Scorned by the guilt, he felt perhaps their allegations were right, and he did deserve criticism. Accepting the blame, he would never forgive himself. For the last three agonizing days, he had stood by, waiting patiently, as Rachel was laid out in her home. Brokenhearted, he could do nothing else except think of her. She was on his mind, in his heart, and within the depths of his soul.

On the last day of her wake, she was taken to the Church of the Divine where her Mass of Commemoration was held and the eulogy was presented by Reverend Peterson. The brothers, who had nothing to add to their sister's eulogy, sat silently wallowing in their own guilt, reminded of their complicity.

At least one good thing did occur from this unsettling event and that was the compassion Rachel's father showed toward his daughter. Shocking all who surrounded him, he proved to everyone he was not at all that gruff man and did have a heart inside him. Breaking down hysterically for the first time in his life, he poured out his heart as he sobbed uncontrollably over her coffin. His sons were surprised, never having witnessed their father act in such a way. He always portrayed himself as the stern, hard father who stood like the Rock of Gibraltar. Out of his three children, Rachel was his favorite without contest, being the youngest and only female of his offspring. Although it may not have appeared so from his firm image, nevertheless, he held Rachel, named after his mother, in high regard and loved her dearly.

Following the ceremony, her casket was taken outside to the plot in the church cemetery where she would be laid to rest. Again, family and friends gathered to pay their last respects. After the prayers of the dead were read, the flowers were cast and the coffin was slowly lowered into the ground. Rachel's mother, who had stayed strong until now, suddenly broke down at this heart wrenching moment. Deeply affected and overwhelmed, she could not bear the strain and soon passed out from the sight of the coffin being lowered.

Not far off, standing alone at the top of the hill was Shawn who overlooked the field as a spectator of this sad day. He too had been deeply affected. Cradling a nearby tree, he observed the entire affair from a distance. He was not a defiant person who would show disrespect and did as the family insisted by not being a participant. Waiting patiently, he watched until everyone had departed and the attendant filled the hole, finishing his work with his final touches by packing the earth and setting a temporary cross.

Once all were gone, he slowly descended the hill, making his way to Rachel. Stopping before the foot of her grave, he could not hold back the tears that quickly filled his eyes. All that was left was overshadowed by the loss of his love and the yearning he felt for her. Walking over to the side of her cross, he grew weak and fell to his knees. Raising his head, he noted her name etched out in the temporary wooden cross. With his finger he traced over each letter of her name, reminiscing their tender moments together. Unable to control himself, he again sobbed. The pain he felt was agonizing, and at that moment, he wanted to die too. All that he lived for was now gone, and he felt utterly alone.

All that he did, he did for her, and all that he was, he was because of her. If only he could roll back time, he thought, how differently he would do things. He would never stop feeling guilty for the consequences of that day. If he had not suggested they look for trees, she would have been alive today, enjoying themselves as two wildflowers blowing in the wind. It grieved him deeply to think of it, but sad as it was, it was true.

Just then, a light rain began to fall, and he glanced up to the heavens. He was reminded of a simple quote he had heard in events such as these, "Every drop of rain that falls is a tear shed by an angel's sorrow."

He questioned why it had to happen this way, assuming the blame and punishing himself for her death, as well as the baby's. He could not stop the hurt, and for him, life no longer had meaning. Parting the soil above her grave, Shawn dug a small hole with his hands. He wanted to leave a lock of his hair as a symbol that a part of him had died as well. It may have meant very little to most, but to him, it had great significance. Miserable and feeling despondent, he too wanted to die. He could no longer live without her. After all, she was his life, his dreams, and his inspiration, and knowing that he would never set eyes on her again affected him profoundly.

******

The following day Isabel was busy in the kitchen cooking dinner when she was startled by a loud crash and a strong vibration. The disturbance was so noticeable that some of the plaster from the ceiling fell, just missing her as it splattered to the floor. For the life of her, she could not understand what Shawn was doing, so she decided to investigate.

Ascending the steps, her instincts warned her that something was terribly wrong. Accelerating her pace, she threw open the door and was ridden with shock as she found Shawn dangling by the neck in the middle of his room gasping for air. Rushing to his side, she took hold of his legs and tugged upward, frantically trying to relieve the pressure to his neck. She realized she was in a predicament since she was unable to hold up his weight indefinitely. She knew she could not let go for an instant, and yet on the other hand, she somehow had to remove the hangman's noose or he would die. But how? The rope was too high and impossible for her to reach.

All alone with no one to turn to or call, she felt worried and became desperate, resorting to the only alternative she had left and that was her witchery. Closing her eyes, she placed herself in deep concentration as she recited a sequence of words to expel a charm. In the moments that followed, the sky around the mansion grew darker and the wind intensified. The door windows of the bedroom slammed open with such force that they broke the panels within the frames. Simultaneously with the breakage of the glass swooped in five ravens. With their powerful beaks, they pecked vigorously at the rope until each strand of the twine became frayed, dropping Shawn safely into his mother's arms.

Quickly she removed the knot from around his neck, and gasping for air, he took his first breath. Seeing breathing restored, she was grateful to her pets for their rescue and their timely arrival. Struggling with all her might, she dragged Shawn over to his bed and rolled him onto the mattress. Having access to a pitcher of water on the side of his bed, she wet a cloth and wiped his face as he regained consciousness. She was elated to see that he was well, but he needed to rest in order to fully recuperate.

Tenderly she kissed him, assuring him of her presence, and urged him to sleep. Pulling a chair to the side of the bed, she sat, not leaving his side for an instant. She wanted to be there just in case he needed her. While the ravens remained perched across his headboard guarding Shawn, Isabel smiled with delight, mindful of her pets' intervention.

Feeling relief, she sat quietly, surrounded by sheer silence. She was almost able to hear the many thoughts that crept into her mind. As she reflected on Shawn's problems, she felt pity for what had happened to him, realizing now just how deeply Rachel's death had affected him. She was aware that they had loved each other very much and that Rachel was the only person who had brought true happiness into his life.

Never realizing that he was that distraught that he would actually take his own life, she hadn't seen tonight's events coming. He had never said a word nor given any indication of his depression, and she could not understand why he had not originally come to her. If only he had spoken to her, she could have at least eased some of his pain. After all, losing your family could be reason enough to drive you to acts of such madness.

Saddened for Rachel, she felt terrible that her life had ended so suddenly and so young. It saddened her even more as she thought of the baby, knowing she would be deprived of becoming a grandmother. That yearning of immense joy now ceased to exist, and the prospect of those visions was now overshadowed by a bleak and uncertain future.

Unfortunately, she could not do very much with her witchery. Although she possessed certain powers, she was unable to raise the dead and only had the power to prolong life. She hoped that time would heal Shawn's wounds and that eventually he would get over this tragedy. Perhaps he would meet another woman who would rekindle his love, giving him new meaning to go on and forget his sorrowful past.

Yet her thoughts were not only restricted to Shawn. She also contemplated on the troubles she faced, reflecting on her life and the path she had already taken. She had come to realize that she was a changed person whom she no longer knew or liked. So proud of her father, she had wanted to follow in his image, but somehow she had strayed from those valuable, meaningful, and significant virtues, which he so much wanted to instill. Her father, a gentle and caring person, would never have inflicted harm on another person, no matter how angry he became. As she thought on it, to her despair and grave disappointment, she had not become like her father at all.

Although she despised her mother for all she represented, in reality her character had apparently developed into hers, a thought she dreaded. Reviewing her past, she was amazed to discover that she resembled her mother in more ways than she cared to admit. Not having given any real thought to it before tonight, she realized that she had taken on her mother's traits and her legacy for what she was best noted, a murderer. As she further compared herself to her mother, she could see that she had psychologically internalized her attributes by becoming ruthless, sinister, and even had resorted to inflicting harm and, worse yet, death, something she never believed she was ever capable of doing.

Even though she found strength in her rage, she reasoned her rash behavior was all contributed to the protection of her son. Loving him as she did made her resort to taking those drastic measures for his defense. As she tried to ease her conscience and justify her actions, she reasoned she was his mother; she was bound to defend him, regardless of the circumstances. It was because she was unable to bear his suffering or see him injured that prompted her to act. This in itself had triggered an insane impulse within her.

She had never wanted to resort to violence or use her powers of witchery. Without pity, she had dispensed much harm, maiming one and murdering many. Nonetheless, her rampage had not yet ended; there would still be others to follow. This much she did comprehend, and she accepted the burden wholeheartedly.

She yearned for peace, wanting so much to be left alone. Unfortunately, society in its mayhem forbids this from ever being so. Feeling tangled within a web of deception, she was a product of her own making, and there was not very much she could now do to change the tide.

Chapter XVIII

A Family's Doom

Rachel's death had had a rippling effect on her whole family.

Her brothers, who had to live with the burden of killing their sister, were so afraid of exposing their horrible crime that they vowed not to say a word to anyone of what they had done. Keeping true to the family's belief that a stray hunter's bullet had killed their sister by accident, it was not long after her death that they both received their final due.

Three years after Rachel's death, her youngest brother, unable to live with his guilt, committed suicide. He could no longer face what he had done and took his own life with the very same gun used to kill his sister. One night without saying a word, he walked into the barn, placed the barrel into his mouth, and pulled the trigger. He left a note, explaining to his parents of the wrong he had done to Rachel, expressing his sorrowful regrets for his everlasting mistake.

While the older brother, the more dominant one and instigator of the sinister plan, went on to live to a ripe old age in life, if you could call it that. He apparently went crazy and was placed in an insane asylum just after his brother's death. He was haunted by his sister's spirit, seeing her ghost each night as he tried to go to sleep. Affected by insomnia and deeply depressed, his appearance took on that of a pale, old, scrawny man. After all, one would think a fate such as this would happen. How could a conscientious person live when faced with the mere thought of being responsible for killing his own sister?

So frightened out of his wits was he that his eyes bulged from their sockets as he sought to hide in the smallest corner of his padded cell, shouting deliriously from his mad visions. Although the institute kept his light on around the clock, it somehow was not enough to overcome his haunting. Even with the lights on, he could still see his sister's face staring at him in her bloodstained dress, repeatedly asking the tormenting question, "How could you do this to me? I trusted you."

As for Rachel's mother, she was never the same person after the truth came out. Although having always been the only sensible one and the foundation of the family, she fell into a severe state of dejection. Not giving a damn for anyone or anything and giving up on life, she died before her husband from a broken heart.

The father took the death of Rachel extremely hard. While he appeared stern and strong-minded, his demeanor was nothing more than a front, covering up his true nature of a sensitive person whose feelings were easily hurt. Rachel was his favorite. Although his concerns were to protect her the best and only way he knew how, they often clashed, their characters being much the same. Her mother, who loved them both dearly, was the mediator, always ironing out the differences between them. Being high strung, he flared up at the slightest of things, which he always attributed to his Irish temperament. Nevertheless, Rachel was indeed his pumpkin, and when he died shortly after his wife, it was with his final breath that he called out her name.

Yet the folks of Colchester had their own mystical theories about the Thompson family's adversities. Ever since Rachel's death, it was as if a cloud of doom had hung over them where they experienced nothing except hardship and bad times. It was firmly believed that they had been cursed and overshadowed by misfortune, which would explain why each member of the household soon came to a sudden, tragic end.

Chapter XIX

A Bit of Kindness

While Shawn recuperated from his close encounter with death, Isabel catered to his every whim, making sure he fully recovered. A few days after, a knock was heard at the front door. When Isabel responded to the caller, she found Gibbs standing there alone. He seemed jolly and in good spirits, stating that he had important matters and needed to speak to her directly. Invited in, she led him into the parlor where he was asked to be seated while she took a moment to prepare some tea.

As Isabel returned with the tea, Gibbs rose from his seat, a joyous smile beaming across his face. He then proceeded to remove an envelope from inside his jacket pocket and handed it to her. He was happy to announce that all the charges set against her son had been dismissed, and there would be no need for him to appear.

At that instant, she could have hugged and kissed him for delivering such wonderful news but for Isabel that would have been unlady like, so she held her composure. Curious, she expressed her interest, wanting to know more about this delightful revelation. With everything falling into its proper perspective, Gibbs explained his intervention and a new judge's position on the law. The rest had taken care of itself, and the evidence, along with witnesses' accounts, was enough to prove Shawn's innocence to the judge.

She did not know that a new magistrate had been appointed to the Colchester courts. He was unlike his predecessor, the uncle of Shawn's accuser, who had been influenced by family members, manipulated evidence and witnesses' accounts, and deemed their testimony inadmissible in Shawn's case.

Gibbs, who had reviewed the files including the constable's report and eyewitnesses' testimony, concluded after reading all the documents that the judge had suppressed vital information for the defense that was crucial to Shawn's case. Gibbs had felt sorry that he had arrested Shawn for the murder of the prostitutes and felt he owed him that much for wrongly accusing him, taking it upon himself to present the facts to the new magistrate.

He was appalled by the proceedings set in the case and couldn't agree more that there had been an obstruction of justice. After reviewing all the evidence presented to him, the judge saw that Shawn was indeed innocent of the charges and was grateful that Gibbs had brought this matter to his attention.

She could not understand why Gibbs would do such a thing and get involved. Nevertheless, she felt it was decent of him to help her son. It was the first time in a long time that someone had showed her and her family a bit of kindness.

Chapter XX

On a Murderess' Streak

It was the night before Christmas Eve. Isabel was sitting in her parlor warming herself before the fireplace. The fire was radiant and burning brightly, the only light reflecting into the darkest corner of the room. Her mind was full and her heart was heavy as she sat there alone in deep contemplation. She was saddened by the recent events and preferred to be in the dark, concealing the lonely tears that filled her watery eyes.

Lately, during the holiday season, she felt in a gloomy mood. Especially this year with all that had happened, the burden was all too much for her to bear. With Dutch's death, the fatal accident of Rachel and her baby, and her son's attempted suicide, she was driven to the pits of despair, unable to weather the grief.

The only consolation that seemed to help her through her misery was the fond memories of her early childhood. It was moods such as these that made her think of her father, and she could not help herself since they were the highlights of her life.

As she reflected on past holidays, she looked back at the delightful times when she was a young girl. After all these years, the moments which she shared together with her father were still treasured, and she could distinctly remember the fun times as they gathered pine branches to weave Christmas wreaths to hang over the doorways of the entrance and parlor. The large tree, at least ten feet high, towered high above her head, so big that her father needed a ladder just to reach midway to the top, always having his little helper faithfully hand him each ornament to give the tree its special touch.

Clearly, the one thing she recalled the most was the thrill of accompanying her father to London to see the sights. Ahh, what pleasure were these wonderful thoughts, which quickly brought a trace of a smile across her face. They were joyous moments, acting like two children so caught up by the rush of excitement that they did not know which direction to proceed to first. Making their excursions into town, their first stop was the gift shop followed by the storefronts with their seasonal window displays to make one merry and gay. With all the thrills, there was that too of the opera, a must see, which featured its traditional Christmas show. After all the laughter, smiles, and pleasure that a person could bear, their visits were always completed by her father's insistence of buying her favorite treat of roasted chestnuts. Even now at this very moment, the memory was so vivid; it was unable to escape her. With their sweet, fragrant smell, as she roasted some in her open fireplace, was the remembrance of those delicious nuts.

Saddened, her eyes once again filled as she shed some more tears, knowing that those days could never be repeated. Then she was reprieved and consoled by a second thought. If Shawn had not come into her life, her days would have been empty. He gave her days new meaning. He made her feel content, alive, and fulfilled. Now she needed to do the same for him.

She knew they needed something to rekindle that spark in their lives. Suddenly that twinkle of joy glowed within her eyes, and she was energized by the thought that she and Shawn could travel to London and relive those wonderful times that she had once shared with her father. How dumbfounded she felt; the concept had never before crossed her mind and she could not understand why. Perhaps it was because she was so preoccupied with her quandaries of recent events.

She would make it a point next year to fulfill this promise, feeling that by then Shawn would be fully recovered. Together they would restore that inspiration they both lacked in their lives. Undoubtedly, there were other matters that plagued her troubled mind. Feeling unrest, she could not find peace until she was liberated from all that threatened her.

She could not forget Reverend Peterson's incriminating suggestions as he took it upon himself to notify the authorities and expose the intimate secret of Shawn's true mother, giving rise to a prompt investigation into her private affairs. That action alone infuriated her. She considered his meddling inexcusable as he had caused her and Shawn a great deal of mental as well as physical distress. Being a man of the cloth, she would have thought he'd have been more discreet. She was under the impression that a confession was safe, knowing that he was a clergyman who had vowed never to divulge what had been revealed to him. But to her dismay, he had, and she was deeply disturbed by his behavior and felt he had wronged her terribly by not confronting her first before saying a word to anyone else.

Stressed to the limit, she was obsessed by a depraved desire to punish all those who opposed her. Blinded by her visions of retribution, she was no longer in control, losing all sense of rational reasoning and driven by profound and contemptuous anger. Knowing the reverend for what he really was, an intemperate drunk who could not mind his own business, she swore he would pay dearly for his interference.

******

It was one in the morning on Christmas Eve when Reverend Peterson heard a woman's voice call out to him. He had been drinking heavily as he often did at this late hour and felt his mind might be playing a trick on him. To his astonishment, he had not been mistaken at all, as he heard that very voice call out again, this time with intensity and using his first name. Placing down his glass of port, he curiously rose from his chair with candlestick in hand, and he exited the room to investigate the distraction.

Enthusiastically, he headed toward the chapel from where the sound seemed to be emanating. Experiencing dizziness and blurred vision, he had the hardest time selecting the right key to unfix the lock. Once he achieved the opening, he entered the room, falling forward toward the pews and supporting himself against them for a short time before he regained his balance.

Having the notion that someone was in the sanctuary, he extended the candle high above his head to better view his surroundings and announced his presence by calling out to see if anyone was there. Overshadowed by darkness, he wanted to establish additional light. He attempted to transfer his candle's flame to another, but overcome by intoxication, his unsteadiness knocked over the candle stand, causing it to crash to the floor. Again, his attentions were drawn to that voice, and his intuition assured him that the calling came from inside the bell tower. Staggering to cross to the other side, he passed the altar where he reached the bell tower and opened its door.

As he entered, he paused in the center, looking up above his head at the spiral staircase. Continuously it called out his name, and he was compelled to respond, driven by an unknown force, seductive and beckoning him to come. He had no doubt in his mind that she was up in the bell tower. Disproving all theories, he could not understand how she could have gotten there undetected and with all the doors locked. Yet one fact remained in his mind, he was not dreaming or hallucinating. Whoever it was, the voice was real, and she was surely up there waiting for him to come.

Overwhelmed by his anxiousness, he ascended the steps, taking careful strides, making every effort to pull his way up the rope banister. Once he reached the top, he was astonished by what he saw. Rubbing his eyes, he had to look a second time. It was beyond belief.

Standing before him was a woman stark naked, holding out her arms, enticing him to embrace her. Her long, white hair fixed in a French braid, he had never before seen such beauty in a woman, and she rendered him weak and lustful. Ever since his wife's death six years ago, he had been celibate and was now tempted by his strong desire. For an instant, he felt his soul impaired and dangling within the boundaries of limbo. As she approached, he tried to resist her sexual advances, but he grew weaker by the minute as she placed her arms around his neck. But what did he care; he was infatuated by her touch, aroused by her incitement, and he was willing to lose all of his principles in a battle lost to Satan.

She advanced closer, brushing up against his body, and he became instantly stimulated by her contact. He could feel the eagerness build within him, as he wanted her more and more. Standing motionless, he closed his eyes, swooning over the very thoughts of her seductiveness. He was now captivated by her charm and was indeed a prisoner of her will. Gently she caressed his chin, and soon after, he felt the extending strokes upon his neck with the tender touch of her fingers. A kiss to his lips excited him, and the warmth of her body close to his drove him to a wild, passionate desire for the flesh. He could no longer resist and wanted desperately to become intimate. Pressing her body close to his, he leaned back with her resting upon him as he felt a sensation of flying through a cool rush of air that was pleasurable, and he hoped the experience would never end. Then suddenly a violent jerk was felt, and thereafter, the pleasure ended as she vanished, and all he could hear in the darkness was a bell ringing.

******

The disturbing sounds rang continuously, waking up most of the community. It was two in the morning, and they wondered why the bell was ringing at this particular hour of the night. It was not Christmas morning when the bell traditionally sounded the event, clearly calling all to Mass held in commemoration of Christmas Day. There were also other possibilities for why the church bell was sounded, perhaps a call for help needed in a disaster. But this sound was most unusual. Unlike the normal sound where the ringing was more rapid, this sound had a slow beat that paused every few seconds between bongs.

Nevertheless, there were those who respectfully responded to the sound of the bell. Wrapped tightly in their cloaks for a bitterly cold night, the party of men proceeded to find out exactly what this calling was all about.

As they approached the church grounds, they found it unusual that Reverend Peterson was nowhere to be seen nor were the chapel doors unlocked so that they could freely enter once they arrived. The whole procedure was out of the ordinary, and they suspiciously became alarmed.

Not finding the reverend and hearing the bell still ringing, they decided to see if the rectory had been left open. Finding it locked as well, they pounded on the door, but after fifteen minutes, there was still no response. After additional pounding and waiting, they became weary and got the eerie feeling that something was terribly wrong as the bell tolled on.

They took measures upon themselves and forced the door in as they called out to the reverend. He was nowhere to be found in the rectory either, and they widened their search into the chapel, lighting the interior. Upon first inspection, they detected a noticeable disturbance with the splattering of several books and a candle stand knocked onto the floor. Although visibility was poor in the dimly lit chapel, they could see that the door of the bell tower across from them had been left open, and the sound of the bell could still be clearly heard.

As they broadened their search into the bell tower, they found it most peculiar to hear the bell ringing while no one was below pulling on its rope. With curious scrutiny, holding their lanterns high, they entered the tower and were frozen in their tracks as they watched in shock of their remarkable discovery.

To their horror, high above them, hung by his neck, was the Reverend Peterson. Having landed on a crossbeam, his front torso bobbed side to side and acted as a counterweight, ringing the large bell.

At the break of dawn on Christmas Eve, Inspectors Gibbs and Moore were summoned to investigate the tragic death of the reverend. The authorities had intentionally waited until morning's first light to begin conducting the case, making it easier to uncover any evidence or clues.

Once entering the rectory, an immediate check was conducted of all doors and windows, and they were both satisfied to learn that there was no forced entry made other than the one made by the discovery party. As Gibbs made his way into the living room, he stood quietly for a moment as he scanned the area where the reverend had been sitting. Obviously, Reverend Peterson must have been distracted by something. The wine bottle and glass were half-full and the book the reverend had been reading was placed face down on the seat of the chair, clearly marking his page.

Following the path he assumed the reverend had taken, he came to the chapel door to find it open with the key still inserted in its lock. It was there, not far from the entrance, that he discovered the books and candle stand sprawled all over the floor. Passing the altar, he made his way to the bell tower, slowly entering and approaching with caution as he carefully looked for clues. Standing in the middle, it was then, as he gazed up, that he saw the most ghastly of sights. There, high above him, was the reverend, strung out across the beam with eyes bulging and a rope fixed tightly around his neck. The impression was disturbing to him as he remembered having just conversed with him not long ago while he was alive and well.

Ascending the spiral staircase, he stopped short of the last three steps where he saw the burnt down candle and its holder on the floor of the tower's landing. It was obvious that the floor of the tower had not been cleaned for some time. Years of neglect had left a build up of dust and bird debris with the dust particles clearly outlining each step of the reverend's movement. Able to see well enough from where he stood, there was no need for him to go any further. The pattern was strange, he thought. As he stared at the footprints, he tried to visualize a scenario to fit the scene of the crime. As he continued to unfold the mystery, he became further baffled by the evidence, and as an afterthought, he wondered whether the reverend's death could have even been suicide.

He quickly ruled out murder. After all, there was no second set of prints in the dust nor was there any disturbance from a struggle or radical movement to indicate even a violent plunge. All the evidence suggested that the reverend took four steps forward, stopped, and then turned with his back to the bell and the drop. He seemed to have been standing there with his feet together; then the prints showed he must have gently tilted and fell backward with the rope tied around his neck. It was unusual that he would plunge in such a way. If he had decided to commit suicide, the jump made no sense at all. Prior experience led him to believe that the jump would have been forward instead of backward. Besides, there was an absence of a suicide note. This added strength to his theory since he was certain that the reverend, being the man he was, would have left a note stating his troubled mind. But what really struck him as most extraordinary was how the reverend was able to tie the rope around his neck in the first place. The rope, being ten feet away, was literally impossible for him to reach without falling, despite the added disadvantage of having his back to it.

He definitely had a puzzle on his hands, one that disputed all possible theories. No note to clarify a suicide, the rope beyond reach, no presence of a second set of prints to verify murder, and even the possibility of an accidental fall seemed remote due to the simple fact that the rope was tied around his neck.

However, the one thing of which he was certain was the reverend was distracted by something and went to investigate. That much was revealed to him by the evidence. The book and wine gave him that indication. As he saw the book left open, faced down to mark the page, and the unfinished half glass of port, it was obvious that Reverend Peterson had every intention of returning to continue where he left off. He could not substantiate the exact cause of death and that is what made this case so uniquely mysterious.

After Inspector Moore and his department's personnel removed the body from the beam, Gibbs was most anxious to check through the pockets of the deceased to substantiate whether he had indeed left a suicide note there. Unfortunately, there was none. Now he was required to establish probable cause of death. But how could he, when he was uncertain himself? He had no solid proof of the circumstances surrounding the death, only conjectures, and he needed much more before coming to any final determination. Rather than be hasty, for the time being, he would classify the death as inconclusive and label the case still under investigation. This decision would enable him further time to investigate, hoping to uncover a missing clue that would be beneficial in solving the case.

Consequently, the death of the reverend was a big disappointment as well as a major setback. With the concept of the case shedding new light, the moral question was raised as to whom was this mystical murderer. He was clever enough to delude the police, cover up all traces of his presence, and leave the investigation in disarray.

Gibbs had apparently been mistakenly fooled into believing that the case had been solved when Dutch was named as murderer. To his dismay, he now had an inexplicably more diverse challenge, quite the contrary from his original expectations. Thinking back to the magistrate's death along with those of Nancy and Peggy, there, too, were many inconsistencies. Though their deaths were not similar in the brutal way they had been killed, the lack of evidence and the circumstances surrounding the scenes were controversial and deemed mysteriously peculiar. With this added death, he now had new reservations about Dutch as the murderer of the prostitutes and felt perhaps a mistake might have been made.

He was confronted with the knowledge that he was pursuing no ordinary killer. With the chain of deaths credited to him, he showed no pattern, killing at random in such a way that was wild and unusually bizarre to the imagination. He felt toyed with by this particular murderer. Realizing he had never had as much difficulty as he did now, he admitted to himself that for the first time in his life he was baffled. Truly, the case was a quagmire, but he hoped that with time his unrelenting patience would win out over his adversary's endurance.

******

As for Isabel, it was agonizing for her to watch Shawn driven to the pits of despair and devoured by his conscience in self-guilt. She had been worried sick about him for some time now; for ever since Rachel's death and his attempted suicide, Shawn had lost his incentive to live and had fallen into a deep state of dejection. No longer that fun-filled, lively son she had once known, his radical change was so severe that he restricted himself from all pleasures of life and confined himself to the desolation of his room. Lethargic, he did nothing more than sit on his terrace staring at the fields of the countryside.

With a warm smile and an affectionate kiss to express her love, Isabel, faithfully and inconspicuously, made a check on the status of his health each morning. Her mind was tortured with worry over his lack of vitality, and concerned for his well-being, she slaved over a hot stove each day to make sure he received the necessary daily requirements of hearty, balanced meals. Despite her vigorous efforts toward his nutritional upkeep, he met her undying devotions with sheer silence. Unresponsive and laden with emotional pain, he never even acknowledged her presence.

As he wasted away with the passage of time from eating very little, he slowly became the epitome of his own destruction. Discouraged, Isabel realized she had done all that was humanly possible to overturn this terrible trend and make him confront his troubles. Although she had been there for him, her best efforts were futile, and she grieved that she wasn't more persuasive for his salvation. To her dismay, she knew his condition was rapidly deteriorating, and she felt the impending breath of death lingering upon the threshold. Dreading the worst, she knew she had to act decisively to alter this plight soon, for if she failed, the consequences would be too devastating and she would lose him forever. Giving thought to the delicacy of the situation, she felt there was only one thing left for her to do.

******

The following morning, just as the sun peeked over the horizon, Shawn was seated in his usual place, watching the dawn break into a new day. He had been sitting there passively for some time now as had become his routine since he very rarely slept, continually plagued by nightmares that relived Rachel's death in his vivid dreams.

But this morning the dawn seemed a bit unusual, bringing with it a mild westerly wind and the intimacy of a past that was most loved and unforgotten, for behind him he felt the presence of another standing still and silently probing. For some reason he mysteriously knew that it was not his mother but someone else with whom he was well acquainted, and urged by fond memories of the past, his emotions suddenly became stirred. Even though he did not turn to look, unsure and unable to believe his instincts, he puzzlingly questioned whether this notion could truly be possible. Yet it was that distinct smell of gardenia, a familiar scent in her hair, which convinced him that it could be none other than his dear friend Louise.

With delight, he excitedly turned and rose from his chair to see if his intuition was correct. To his insight, a yearning was now revealed, and he could not hold back the tears of joy that quickly filled his eyes. He missed her now more than ever before, needing the comfort of her compassion. Pitifully, she looked at him with passionate eyes, filled by the love that glowed within. She was aware of his depression and wanted to fill that emptiness and do all she could to ease his pain. With the rush of adrenalin, he hastily moved toward her, and she eagerly responded to his advance, locking tightly into a grip of a warm embrace. It was that look, her tenderness, and a recollection of a person both powerful and influential in his life, which instinctively had an impact upon him. Sparked by her sheer presence, along with her effusion of empathy, he soon broke the bonds of his imprisoned heart and alleviated the scars of his tormented soul.

******

As for Isabel, this resolution came to her as a great relief. With Shawn's languishment subsided, the suffering which she endured was now replaced by the restfulness of an eased mind. After all, Louise was his first love, and he had loved her dearly, suffering a broken heart upon losing her on that regrettable day. She looked very much like Rachel, practically being her twin, and Isabel had no doubt that with the passage of time Shawn's love would be rekindled.

Her decision to return Louise was apparently the right choice. The past two days were a testament of his dramatic convalescence, and his incentive for living had been once again restored. Extending his boundaries beyond his room, Louise's powers of persuasion were overwhelming. She aroused and inspired him into a recovery, and where he had once experienced the worst, he was now fulfilled by the inspiration of her love.

Assured that Louise would occupy Shawn for the immediate future, Isabel, free from her duties of nursing him, could now once again fully concentrate on her desires. Pointing her finger of scorn with contemptuous infliction, it was forthcoming and conceivable that Isabel would make her assault very soon.

With the reverend being one more adversary out of the way, it was very probable that Moore would be her next objective. If there ever was a person she truly wanted to harm, it surely was Moore. She had never forgotten the cruelty and brutality he had shown her son on the day of his arrest and worse still his contumelious behavior as he taunted Shawn while he callously exposed the hardened truth of his roots and abandonment. Her hatred was profound, lingering in the midst for some time, waiting patiently for the right moment to make her move, and now with the congregation at the reverend's funeral, she felt the time could not be more appropriate.

******

Stressed by urgency, the church in its haste readily dispatched the Reverend Calvin Potts. For now, he would be the new pastor for the Colchester parish and perform the Christmas services as well as the requiem for the late Reverend Peterson. Because he arrived late on the evening of Christmas Day, the annual Mass did proceed with some delay, celebrating the holiday service the next day with the burial for the reverend to follow the day after.

On the last day of the reverend's wake, the attendance for the morning's Mass was expected to fill the chapel to capacity. With a variation of moods from somber to curious, there were also, of course, the instigators with their many theories and speculations on how the reverend died and who placed much of the blame on witchery as the vital cause. Having a better than expected flock of parishioners, friends, and relatives, it was to everyone's surprise when the incomparable Inspector Gibbs and his assistant Inspector Moore paid their final respects.

Gibbs had a suspicion that the murderer might attend the burial, and he wanted to be there to observe the event, satisfying his inner gut feeling. He secretly hoped that perhaps with a bit of luck a development would occur where the killer would expose himself by some sort of outburst or have a contemptuous facial expression displaying his animosity.

After the Mass, the pallbearers hoisted the coffin and the funeral procession moved outdoors to its final destination, soon reuniting the reverend with his dear wife. Although it was winter, the reverend's plot was in the most beautiful section and setting of the church's burial ground. Surrounded by various trees consisting of cherry, crabapple, and dogwood, the display was wondrous with an array of colors when the first sign of spring made its appearance.

As the coffin was propped up above the open excavation and supported by a few beams, the faithful assembled as the Reverend Potts proceeded with the prayers and the opening of the eulogy. With careful scrutiny, Gibbs surveyed the mourners, watching their reactions closely, reading each of their sad and drawn faces. However, there was not one who he could determine showed the slightest resentment toward the reverend. To his disappointment, it appeared that the killer had not made his appearance. If he had, he was very much in control, quite inconspicuous, and successful in suppressing his contempt.

With the conclusion of the eulogy, the coffin was slowly lowered into the ground while several mourners, ridden with grief, poured out their aching hearts, vented by the depletion of their sorrowful tears. Each, in turn, took a handful of earth, and as they passed the pit to express a final farewell, the dirt was tossed into the hole, symbolizing their respect, love, and admiration. After the ceremony, the community sponsored a short, friendly convocation at the sacristy, where tea and muffins were served to all who had attended the burial.

Moore, who had arrived with Gibbs in his buggy, decided to return to town, needing to catch up with some unfinished paperwork that had accumulated. However, Gibbs remained behind wanting to mingle with the group in hopes of finding a lead and would later hitch a ride back to town with the Bakers.

Just a fifteen-minute ride to town, the road was slippery with patches of ice along the way, especially by the stream's bridge where the build up of ice had accumulated from the mist of the falls. Moore in his haste did not take the vital caution he should have by proceeding slower than usual just to avoid any mishap that could occur under these treacherous conditions.

Little did he know that Isabel's pets were already dispatched, all silently perched in the tree by the bridge's crossing, patiently awaiting his arrival. For some time now her ravens had been following him, knowing of their objectives, inconspicuously hidden from view until the detection of his presence would render him alone and isolated from any witnesses.

With a flip of a whip, he galloped down the straight, heading for the bend in the road just before the foot of the bridge. At that particular moment, he saw, off at the horizon, a flock of black birds heading toward him backed by an overcast sky. He thought nothing of this sighting until they closed the distance and flew at a much lower altitude, seeming to head right for him. Not expecting to be on a collision course, he was caught off guard as the lead bird suddenly swooped down on him. With a quick response, he darted to the side, avoiding a piercing of his face, and instead was slapped by the force of its wings as it flapped away. Simultaneously with the lead bird's dive, the pack followed in pursuit, causing a frenzy of confusion, and he was aghast as he realized he was under attack. The concentration of their pecking seemed to be directed at his eyes, and waving his arms wildly about, he tried desperately to ward off any more injury to his face. He knew he was in crisis and could not understand what he had done to provoke them. Yet he was sure of one thing and that was his afflictions and the pain he was now suffering. Still under the flogging attack and distracted from his whereabouts, Moore did not notice he was approaching the sharp bend in the road. With an increase of speed, the horse cut the sharp turn, and unable to hold its stability, the wagon slid and screeched across the ice-covered cobblestone. The pavement like a sheet of ice caused the wagon to slam against the stone parapet with such force that it bounced to one side tossing Moore completely over the bridge wall.

After the catered affair, Gibbs, receiving his ride back to town with the Bakers, noticed on his approach an abandoned buggy blocking the road to the river's crossing. As John Baker brought his carriage to a screeching halt, Gibbs turned, and as he made eye contact, he raised a brow, expressing a puzzled look. With his curiosity now aroused, he jumped from his seat to inspect the buggy, only to realize it was his and with Inspector Moore nowhere to be found. Extending his search, he saw the wheel marks that slid across the ice and the stone debris from the damaged wall. Walking over to the point of the accident, he observed the disturbance of snow, which appeared to be pushed off the surface of the wall. For no apparent reason, he leaned over the wall and gazed down, only to be horrified by his discovery. There below him to his sickened stomach was Moore, face up and impaled on the pointed bars of the wrought iron fence. He felt a rush of blood rise in his head as he excitedly scampered down the embankment leading to the bridge base. There he paused before the body, ridden with disbelief as he tried to make sense of the incident.

Stretched out before him, dangling high on an eight-foot fence with spikes piercing through his back and his legs was Inspector Moore, although Gibbs was unable to see the front of his face well. He rationalized that there was no need to make an examination for life. He could tell he was dead from the complexion of his skin and noted that the bleeding had already stopped. Aware there was not very much he could do on his own, he shouted up to John Baker and instructed him to notify the authorities while he remained behind. As he waited, he descried the grounds about him, and his attention was suddenly drawn to the distinct shape of those black feathers.

Apparently, he had not noticed them at first through the rush of excitement. His adrenalin was heightened, for the more he looked, the more he saw; a multitude of feathers was all over, especially around the body where the concentration was the heaviest. During this time, the recovery party arrived, and with Gibbs' direction, they proceeded with the delicate task of removing the body from the fence, using the leverage of several ropes, a pulley, and a ladder. Suddenly their attentions were drawn to a loud blood-curdling shout from the panicked man who stood on the ladder crying out, "Oh, God. Look at this!"

Gibbs knew something was terribly wrong just from the sound of this man's quivering voice and the fright that registered from his enlarged eyes. Soon after the outburst, Gibbs and several men gathered around the body to see what had caused the ladder man to become so distressed.

As the body was lowered down from the hands of the ladder man, the horror was soon revealed. There, to everyone's paralyzing shock, was the most ghastly of sights. Moore's eyes had been pierced right out of his sockets. It was like déjà vu. Gibbs recalled its similarity to the bizarre death of the magistrate, remembering well the black feathers also present at that crime scene.

At first he had felt it was nothing more than an accident case but once seeing Moore's eyes gouged out, the scenario changed to murder. He distinctly remembered noticing during his panic as he ran down the embankment where Moore had fallen that there were no other prints in the snow except his own. He assumed Moore had to be alive up to the point of the bridge accident and had impaled himself as he fell over the wall. The evidence of the damaged wall, disturbed snow, and the skid marks made that all clear.

He could not understand what was the motive behind this awful tragedy; was it a chase, or a trap, and where did the murderer hide? All those puzzling questions repeated over and over in his mind. What also troubled him was how it was possible for the murderer to remove

Moore's eyes without ever showing a trail of prints leading to his body. Nevertheless, the facts spoke for themselves; it was clear that the eyes were removed while he was impaled on the fence. The fragments of the skin tissue and the bloodstains below his head indicated that the murderer had extracted the eyes during the two hours that elapsed while Moore was in the very same position he had been found. What was also baffling was the mere fact that not one streak of evidence could substantiate the killer's presence—only the consistency of feathers, black feathers at that.

With Dutch's death and Shawn ruled out as the murderer, his list of suspects ran thin. As his perception broadened, he began to look at the case from a different perspective. He knew he had made mistakes in the past by accusing the wrong people. Apparently, the murderer was far more clever than he had anticipated.

Revamping his theory, he now had a suspect in mind who had the motive and the potential to be the murderer of many of those victims, and within the dawn of his thoughts, he was astounded by the very idea that this person could have such capabilities. As the puzzle unraveled, the mayhem of the event again dominated the scene, and his thoughts were drawn back to those feathers, lots and lots of feathers. He concluded that the feathers somehow held the key to the mystery and unsolved answer.

As he focused on the black feathers, the birds came to mind. He remembered the day well some time ago when he had his first talk with Isabel at her home. The memory of the five ravens, all perched on her entrance gate, peering at him, intensely watching his every move, had made such an impression that he never forgot it. Then the group was seen again, spread out over his carriage at the moment he and Moore departed from Isabel's home. It was weird, he felt. It appeared as if those birds were purposely following him. It now became clearer as he thought on the subject, and when his hypothesis was applied to the scene of the crime, it made a whole lot of sense in solving the unexplainable. Though it was far-fetched, he could not rule out the possibility while keeping an open mind.

Wildly thinking, he conjectured that perhaps the birds were trained to kill on command, but how could that be, casting much doubt. He had never heard of a bird being that intelligent to carry out a crime, to know of an assignment, and to execute an objective on command. Then suddenly the unthinkable arose, and he felt his hands tremble a bit knowing it disputed all of his beliefs, he being a man of science. Arriving at this conclusion, he felt a diabolical force was at hand. Since the birds were incapable of such activities on their own, they had to be controlled or possessed. He began to wonder and questioned whether it was indeed possible that the birds could be bewitched in order to do someone's bidding. Reluctantly, he was inclined this time to believe his feelings. After all, it would account for all the mysterious events that took place at the scenes of the crimes and why there never was any evidence of a human suspect found anywhere.

He laughed at himself, noting his foolish mistakes, as he came to realize it was not a man he was seeking after all but a woman. He felt he was on the right track this time and was confident that the killer was none other than Isabel Laughton. So sweet, charming, and petite, who would ever think she was capable of such hideous crimes? Yet the answer had always been there as the townsfolk, with their many accusations, pointed the finger of blame on her for witchery. He had felt, at the time, that they were nothing more than a lynch mob, fueled by their jealousy and hatred toward the wealthy, and because of his principles, he had refused to believe in their depraved ways of thinking.

There were also several things she had said and done that drew him to this conclusion. He knew of her lie after the reverend informed him of who Shawn's mother really was. It became too much of a coincidence that shortly after their visit Peggy and Nancy turned up dead. He was sure that Shawn had played a role, being in the middle of a confrontation where Isabel felt threatened and had to dispose of them. There was even that vivid conversation which they had over the magistrate's death that seemed most peculiar when she used the term "plucked out" when describing the extraction of his eyes. At first, he had thought her use of such a term was strange but dismissed it quickly, feeling she had made an error in speech. However, after some considerable thought, she was quite right in assuming the birds, using their powerful beaks, had plucked out his eyes. This would also explain the strange wounds on the face and the black feathers, which were all so noticeable but disregarded. Nevertheless, what was even more of a surprise to Gibbs was how she knew of the horrible way the magistrate had died, considering that very detail was never revealed to the public. Even at the wake, the family to ensure secrecy and to spare the distress of a gruesome sight displayed a closed coffin to all the mourners.

It was her own indication of the knowledge that exposed her guilt, and for some unknown reason, he had overlooked it in the past, feeling it had been nothing more than coincidence. Then again, he blamed himself, perhaps it was his fault for not seeing it. He should have trusted his first instincts. He could not explain why but he felt physically attracted to her. Even though she was much older than he was, she still was a very beautiful woman, and he felt his attraction to her was a grave error on his part.

He realized now with whom he had to contend and knew he was not dealing with an ordinary person. From what he had already witnessed, she was someone quite dangerous who supposedly had the powers of the supernatural. Although she could be lethal, he did not believe she was a psychopath or psychotic where her behavior was out of touch with society.

Preferring not to make an issue of her arrest, he felt a back-up force to be unnecessary nor did he want to alarm her with the presence of a paddy wagon. He instead wanted to approach Isabel alone, sending her a signal that he had come on common ground. A show of force would not have made any difference since she was very capable of defending herself from any threat that may have been imposed on her. The one thing he did not want to do was provoke her or force her into a confrontation. Having already spoken to her on several occasions, he thought she was still quite the lady, and being a good judge of character, he felt the best way to handle this matter was by mutual conversation. He was sure that once he confronted her with the crimes, and with a little bit of persuasion, she would surrender quietly without resistance. After all, she did show her gratitude on the day her son's case was dismissed and on the day of Shawn's arrest when he had intervened and stopped Moore from using excess force.

He was relying largely on his role played out as Good Samaritan, feeling she would be obligated to him for his deeds and would reciprocate by providing no opposition. Nevertheless, whether his theory was true or not, he would never know for sure until he confronted her and took her into custody, regardless of the consequences.

Chapter XXI

One's Regret

At the peak of day, Gibbs rose from his bed, having experienced a restless night with disturbed sleep from being overly concerned about the outcome of today's proceedings. Taking precautions in the event of his probable death, he prepared a note, and after sealing it in an envelope, he placed it in his briefcase where he kept his personal records of the investigation.

The letter was addressed to Scotland Yard expressing his theories and suspicions of a murderer whom he revealed by name and the reasons for taking this homicidal person into custody alone. He was aware of the explosive dangers that could easily erupt in this town and wanted to keep a lid on the arrest knowing his resources were limited. He had even gone so far as to be extra prudent, distrusting the local police, feeling that once Isabel was implicated as the murderer, the news would spread through town like wildfire and touch off a storm of retribution in the community. The local people intolerant and blindly prejudiced about this particular woman would be eager to react. This was part of the reason he chose to adopt his lone plan. Knowing the hatred felt by the townsfolk, he deemed it necessary to be discreet to keep it under control. Gravely concerned, he wanted to avoid a mob that would eagerly turn this case into a witch trial in the form of a burning stake. These by no means were his intentions, and in order to insure her safety from the clutches of an unruly crowd, he was willing, if necessary, to transport her back to London where she could obtain a fair and decent trial. If he believed in anything, it was justice, and despising a lynch mob, he would take extreme measures to ensure a prisoner's safety, regardless of guilt or conviction.

Arriving at Isabel's home that early morning, he was instantly aware that his presence had somehow been expected. Finding the front door wide open, a voice emanated at his entry, calling out to him by name, warmly inviting him to step into the parlor. From the brisk corridor, he entered the heated room. There he observed a radiant fire that had been burning to take out the morning chill with Isabel sitting comfortably in her armchair with her back to him. She did not say another word upon his entrance, but as he approached closer, she made her feeling known, taunting, "You somewhat disappoint me. I was actually expecting your visit much sooner."

It was that incriminating statement that convinced him of her unquestionable guilt as he realized she knew well the purpose of today's visit. Startled by her keen insight, he casually sat alongside her and smiled cordially as he slid himself onto the seat of the sofa.

Turning to face him, she paused for a spell, making eye contact as she teased in a low voice, "You look a bit nervous this morning, Inspector. Do I make you feel that way?"

Declaring, "No, not at all," Gibbs remained composed, and not admitting his true feelings, he tried his best to conceal his fear, hoping not to show weakness in the face of his opponent. Again, the mood of silence arose. With a surge of apprehension, he expected the calm to soon erupt into a fury. It would not be long before the smiles would cease and the silence would soon end.

Gibbs, deciding to have the first word, felt it to be a good time as any to get right to the point and inform Isabel of her arrest. He was aware the news would not sit well with her, and she would probably react in a way to make her discontent known. Whatever the backlash might be, he was unsure, but he hoped the outcome would not be nasty and she would surrender quietly to him without resistance. However, those thoughts were only wishful thinking and he expected far from the truth. In any case, he was prepared for the worst. This moment was the most critical. He had no indication what to expect, realizing he was now putting her back against the wall.

Uneasy, he could feel his hands trembling, and accompanied by a cold sweat, his face grew pensive. He knew from previous crimes the swift action she took against those who defied her and how she retaliated to threats, dispensing death to the peak of perfection. Having witnessed each and every one she had dealt with in her own bizarre way, he worried for his own preservation since now he had become the existing threat.

Pondering his thoughts, his mind wandered, and speculating his fate, he questioned what would be his destiny. Would he be fortunate enough to see the sun rise tomorrow or be damned, cursed to live out a life of blindness, stricken to a world of darkness and driven by despair to dwell in the obscurity of the unknown, feeling one's way about? Or would he be ridden like a vegetable, restricted to go no further than the boundaries of his bedpost, and tormented daily by the thoughts of his decrepit body, deprived of the pleasures of movement and freedom? Or perhaps she would be merciful and just strike him dead in the very spot where he stood, sparing him the agony of a life long suffering. All those thoughts and more ran rampant in his mind.

But before he could open his mouth and announce his intentions, Isabel rudely cut him short, insisting he permit her to have the first say. Gibbs had no qualms about allowing her that privilege, reasoning, perhaps, much might be revealed and a confession might easily be obtained.

Prudently, she displayed an insight into her diversity. She highlighted her love for her son, which she felt Gibbs could never comprehend, and made it known that Shawn was her life, and her life revolved solely around him. It was love from the first day she had set eyes upon him, and once she had cradled him in her arms, she could never let go. He was the answer to her deepest yearnings, and she saw that her destiny was to love him and be his mother thereafter. Once that bond became an affection of a mother's love, there could be no separation between them. "I would first separate my arm, my leg, even my life, but never my son. I would kill for him if I had to," she exclaimed bitterly, wearing a stony expression.

She did not expect Gibbs to understand a mother's point of view, but she did expect him to understand her motives and why she was forced to kill those who imposed harm or robbed her of her son. "Who are they to judge us? Who are they to mock and persecute us?" flushed in the face, she shouted in defiance, referring to the townsteaders.

Driven by necessity, she was motivated to protect her son in the only way she knew how. Even if it resulted in their deaths, that was their misfortune, but justifiable for her self-preservation, feeling she had every right. She admitted, at times, in her rage, she was blinded by the truth and felt nothing but anger and hatred toward those who showed oppression, escalating the situation. Being hurt, betrayed, and persecuted, she learned to adjust and become strong in a society that despised her. She could not help feeling it was because of her reputation that the community isolated her son as a way to get back at her.

Pausing to take a deep breath, she felt Gibbs was unsympathetic, and she grew annoyed that he could not understand her reasoning as to why she took the law into her own hands, becoming judge, jury, and executioner. Bitterly proclaiming with a crack in her voice, "You saw for yourself. Do you truly believe my son would have gotten a fair trial in this town?"

It was with tragic truthfulness she openly revealed her crimes, admitting to each murder and how she carefully planned and executed each person in a way that was similar to the offenses committed in their association to her and Shawn. She remembered it well, the pain she endured on that day when family members influenced the magistrate. Being corrupt and not seeing justice prevail, she decided to blind him as punishment for not seeing the truth, which soon after resulted in his death.

As for the three boys, their innocence was lost at the moment of their unprovoked and vicious attack, inflicting pain upon Shawn, as they thought nothing of the merciless beating they dispensed. Fumed and feeling sorrow for her son's persecution, she swore a mother's revenge for the suffering they had administered, and she made sure they would suffer tenfold an agonizing death.

Never before had she conveyed her heartfelt feelings as she did on the day of Nancy and Peggy's visit. Overwhelmed by their aggressive attitudes and threats to take Shawn away from her, they expected her to just disregard fifteen years of a mother's devotion. Outraged by the mere thought, she felt robbed of a love that was her meaning for life. Driven by anger and desperation, she lost control and felt they instead should be robbed, not of the love they knew nothing about but of their miserable and despicable lives.

As for the town prostitutes, it was their own admission of the truth which made them so much of a danger. Already being close friends in their affiliation with Nancy as ladies of the night and knowing much of her life, they were aware of the birth as well as the abandonment. It was that token of knowledge that made them a threat to her, and as the opportunity arose, driven by necessity, she had to erase their knowledge by silencing that threat once and for all.

At the moment of Reverend Peterson's disclosure, she felt the repercussions of his betrayal. Tempted by an unsettled mind, he eagerly informed Gibbs of her intimate secret, revealing Shawn's true mother. This in itself was unforgivable, and as far as she was concerned, being a man of the cloth, he had broken his vow by not being discreet. Disturbed by that contemptible action, she chose his weakness of temptation as a form of murder to delude and lure him to a definitive doom.

When it came to Inspector Moore, she found nothing more upsetting than the mere mention of his very name. Motivated by his mannerism of aggression, which marked him from the very beginning, Moore, being a repulsive snob who saw himself above others, felt little or no compassion toward the meek, and with superiority over those he belittled or disparaged, he found pleasure in others' misery and despair.

Having lost her respect for him, she was forever reminded of his intentional humiliation and how he had tormented Shawn with the agonizing truth of his bitter roots. It was that cruel and harsh temperament that gave her the incentive to impale him and make him suffer in such a way that was equally as cruel and harsh as his intolerable self.

There was also the Thompson family who had been scorned by Isabel's revenge. It was surprising to Gibbs as she revealed her involvement in their misfortunes and the atrocities of a chain of events that would eventually lead to their deaths. This curse played out over a period of time, ensuring each member of the household to be doomed by the events of the past and to spend each day in the madness of a tormented mind. It was for that memory of Rachel alone that paved their destinies to live out their lives in damnation, cursed and driven to their graves by the admission of their own unsettled hauntings.

He did not understand why she was confiding in him and explaining all in vivid detail. Nor did he realize that she was unafraid and was setting a tone and pace for a confession. She felt Gibbs, being an intellectual, would clearly understand her motives. She knew she was at the helm and in control, and regardless of what he felt to the contrary, she also knew there was very little he could do to stop her.

******

For all practical purposes, she actually did like him. She found him to be mild mannered, not pushy, and quite a gentleman. It was unfortunate that he was a detective and had come to arrest her for those hideous crimes. After all, he was very brilliant in his line of work as a young and prominent man of twenty-five. Only a ten-year difference from Shawn, she could not help feel a motherly instinct toward him.

It was a pity it had to end this way. She never anticipated it would come to this and felt some leniency to spare his life. She would always remember Inspector Gibbs as a gentle man and would never forget the kindness he had once shown her son. Regretfully, this was one of the hardest decisions she ever had to make, and now with this disclosure, she had no alternative but to dispense with him, even though her heart felt differently.

Feeling admiration, she owed him the benefit of the doubt and wanted to give him an opportunity to recant his principles for a more decisive alternative. Not having any real intentions of harming him, she felt that in all fairness she would offer him a proposition. If only he would set aside his differences, discontinue his investigation, and allow the case to remain unsolved, she reflected with thoughts of hope for acceptance of her proposals. But once the alternative was presented, her eyes grew narrow with annoyance, frustrated that he did not see things her way.

In good conscience, Gibbs could not accept her terms, and because of his reluctance, she felt a small demonstration of her power was needed to convince him. Walking to the mantel, she struck a match; lighting a candelabra and carrying it back with her, she set it down on the table between them.

With a closed fist, Isabel raised her hand before his face, symbolizing her hold upon him. Fixed with sharpened eyes and mouth tightened, she uttered a series of words beneath her breath. Just barely able to hear her, he deduced the language to be some sort of Latin chatter. Within the moments that followed, he jumped to his feet, noticing a rush of dark clouds that suddenly blocked out the sun, making all still and silent. With the candelabra the only light in the cover of darkness, he now bore witness as the silence broke and the wind intensified, whirling and sounding the chimes that were strung up across the porch. Astonished by her powers of witchery, she had, in an instant, now transformed this man of science into a firm believer.

From the disturbance of the rattling windows, he turned to face Isabel, and locking eyes, he observed the hideous smirk across her face. Suddenly, he felt a rapid change come over his body, and his eyes grew widely alarmed, tense, and horrified that the worst was yet to come.

Drained pale, he experienced dizziness, and beads of perspiration formed across his entire face. She toyed with him, holding a clenched fist, and with every squeeze of her hand, he felt the sharp pain increase in his chest. Simultaneously, his pressure rose and he could feel his veins pulsating, and as his condition escalated, he began to feel shortage of breath. By now breathing became extremely heavy, and overcome by weakness, he was no longer able to stand. With his eyes taking on a wounded look, he fell back and collapsed against the couch. Bewildered, he soon realized that he was suffering from a heart attack. He was trapped in a paralyzed body, rendering him very little ability to move and speak.

Still having his wits about him, he saw it took very little effort for Isabel to bewitch someone, and he wondered why she had not killed him yet. Making a final plea, she approached him, and squatting down before him, she pitifully stroked him tenderly, imploring him once again to submit to her terms.

Stubbornly shaking his head no, he rejected her pleas. She knew if her demonstration had not altered his ways, he would never give in to her, being a man of principles, pride, and integrity. Forcing her hand, she was left with no choice but to deal with him. Moving her palms across his face in circular motion, she cast a charm, placing him into a deep sleep. After all, she did not have it in her heart to kill him and felt it would be less stressful if she resorted to some other means of control.

In order for her to possess him, she required a part of his body. Returning from the kitchen with cleaver in hand, she chopped off his right index finger to the middle knuckle and wrapped it in parchment paper, which was marked with symbols of the pentagram. For safekeeping, she placed the joint in a small brass box under lock and key. Casting a spell over him, she now placed him in a state of amnesia. Until the day the finger was burnt and destroyed in a flame of fire, Inspector Gibbs would remain in this state for as long as needed for Shawn to live out his life peacefully. Thereafter, she would no longer care, and if Gibbs happened to still be alive, he would be returned to his natural state, remembering more than was ever revealed. But first she had to make sure that before he was discovered, all of his personal records of the case were destroyed, leaving the investigation unsolved and in virtual disarray.

******

The following day Gibbs was seen wandering the streets of the town. Looking a bit ragged, he seemed to be acting peculiar. Unresponsive, he walked aimlessly about, leading the community to sense that something was terribly wrong, and so they contacted the town's constable, reporting the strange behavior. After approaching him and bombarding him with a variety of questions, he quickly realized that Inspector Gibbs was suffering from acute memory loss. He did not know who he was or where he was going. All he did know was that he was very hungry.

Upon further inspection, it was observed that he had a rather serious wound on his right hand. His hand full of blood, it was quite obvious to the officer that Gibbs was missing a part of his finger, although Gibbs did not seem to be in any pain, nor did he even know how he had sustained such an injury. As far as the police were concerned, they did not have the faintest idea what had happened to him and found the whole situation quite bizarre.

Nevertheless, Gibbs was brought to his lodging, and seeing to his only complaint, he was fed a hearty breakfast to ease his hunger. In the meantime, a thorough search was conducted of his room to retrieve his personal records of the investigation. Unfortunately and strangely enough, the only thing they discovered was an empty briefcase and a pile of burnt ashes left simmering in the fireplace.

It was assumed that Gibbs' records of the cases had been destroyed in the fire, and the authorities could not understand why he had done such a thing. With the investigation now overshadowed by the loss of records, besides the inspector's uncanny state, the local police, whose force was made up of only two personnel, were unable to reach any real conclusion as to what had caused Gibbs to suddenly suffer such a strange phenomenon. To the police, the occurrence was quite extraordinary, and when the events were unable to be logically explained, they resorted to a more pessimistic way of thinking, blaming the whole affair on bewitchment.

Helpless as an infant, Gibbs was unable to reason, think, or even perform the simplest of tasks. Once brilliant, he was now a total invalid. With his mind wiped clean, he was unfit to continue his duties as an investigator and was transferred back to London, where he was placed in an institution for further evaluation.

This, of course, had its own repercussions, setting back the Yard and placing the investigation in disarray, with all evidence lost and leads already gone cold. Gibbs' memoirs were a valuable resource and a great asset toward the ability to solve the cases; not only were they the only complete records of the investigation, but they were also testimony to every event and murder that had taken place. Not trusting the local police and while in the heat of the pursuit, Gibbs had safeguarded his records by keeping his findings confidential and away from the snooping eyes of the public.

In his personal memoirs, Gibbs had recorded each murder in its exact detail and the awkward way each one of the victims had mysteriously died. He had included the abnormalities of the crime scenes, conjecturing his own personal feelings and findings, which were contrary to the evidence despite the scientific backing and rational explanations. With a list of suspects whom he had discredited, he also revealed in his text his theories of the case and the unorthodox approach that he took toward a subject who he believed was responsible for the dreadful crimes.

Although it was considered a bit too late, the Yard reassigned another team of investigators to follow up where Gibbs presumably had left off. Unfortunately being three months after the case had gone cold, their expectations did not turn out as they had anticipated, and the investigation was left at a virtual dead end. Despite the many deaths involved, not a single soul was brought before the law to be prosecuted, placing this case in the archive files of the unsolved.

******

"After sixty-four years of living my life as an invalid, my residence here at the Carfax Nursing Home suddenly came to light with my recovery just eight years ago. Prior to that day, I did not know a thing, but as soon as my awakening came about, my mind was haunted by the past, filled with the events of many crimes that had long been forgotten by decades of time. It was surprising to me as well how I remembered so vividly those remarkable accounts and was able to recollect each case and every exact detail of its context. It even frightens me that my memory was more than I had experienced, and I felt a great urgency, compelling me to explain my story, giving me relief knowing that the burden of truth was revealed."

Reeled with astonishment, Margaret had worn down the points of six sharpened pencils; now sitting there silently stunned, she gawked in disbelief from the tale, which she had just heard. Unfortunately, there was no way she could account for the accuracy of Gibbs' story or verify any of the details for truth. With recollections as graphic as he had just told, she could not believe he could make up such a story if it had not been true. It seemed to her that his chronicle of the events made perfect sense, and he had convinced her that he had indeed lived through this ordeal, or he was one hell of a great storyteller, having a wild and considerable imagination.

Nevertheless, Margaret was not quite satisfied as yet and had questions of her own, which she desired to have answered. She wondered what had ever become of Shawn and Isabel and if Gibbs' recovery in 1944 meant that Shawn had died at the age of seventy-five, and if so, where he was buried.

Gibbs did not know for sure the answers to the questions Margaret put to him but due to the fact of his recovery, he believed that Shawn must have passed away. As for Isabel, it was very unlikely that she would still be alive, considering she would be one hundred twenty-five years old by now. It was very probable that they would have been buried in the family vault, which was located somewhere on their estate.

Intrigued by Gibbs' narration, blended superbly with episodes of the supernatural, Margaret believed she was on one hell of a great story and now only needed to photograph the gravesites to finalize her exclusive.

Thanking Gibbs for this wonderful interview, she jumped reflexively to her feet, ready to dash off, realizing that she had spent the entire day there wrapped up in an incredible story. With evening upon her, she expressed her thanks once again, overly apologetic for having taken so much of his time, and assured him that once the story was in print, she would return with a copy of her book.

Chapter XXII

The Investigation

Following up with her investigation, Margaret wanted to photograph and see first hand the estate as well as Shawn's and Isabel's graves. At first light the following morning, she set out on her adventure from London to Colchester. After her three-hour drive, she stopped at the Rocklin Inn only to find that the establishment had since been changed to the Witch Hour Inn.

Isabel had now become a legend around these parts, and with all the publicity, murders, and witchery that had occurred, the inn decided that a new name was needed to keep up with the times. Taking full advantage of Isabel's legacy, the idea was a smart move for the inn. Business boomed, attracting the adventure seekers, the curious, and those, of course, who enjoyed a good witch tale. With the stories of the supernatural to stir up one's imagination, whether it was believed to be myth, legend, or truth, excitement ran rampant in the complex, becoming the prime topic of discussion, exploiting Isabel's presumed murders and curses which she placed on the people of the town in 1891.

Grace, who was young, unmarried, and prominent, was the new proprietor of this establishment and the granddaughter of the previous owners. She knew everything there was to know about Isabel, told to her by her grandparents, and her gift of gossip helped her become prosperous and gain great success. Although Isabel had never been prosecuted for a single murder due to the lack of evidence, it was always suspiciously believed that she had been behind all the crimes committed.

Margaret, after an extensive talk with Grace who was more than happy to share what she knew, gained quite an earful of information of which she was not at all familiar. Among the extraordinary circumstances that surrounded the Laughton family was Isabel's strange disappearance. She had not been seen or heard of for some time now, and it was assumed that she had just passed away.

Shawn's tragic end came in 1944 during the war where he died from an explosion of a V2 rocket that had been driven off course, mutilating him beyond recognition. The servant of the house who heard the massive explosion also was the one to discover his decapitated body. She was under strict instructions that upon his demise she was to notify Shawn's lawyer immediately to actuate his will.

Prepaid for their services, the undertaker and lawyer were met on the estate by an elderly woman dressed in black who wore a veil that concealed her face. This mysterious woman, claiming to be a distant relative, stood by to see that all of Shawn's wishes were carried out to the letter. Specified in his will were directions outlining it to be very private, with no wake, and for him to be placed in a vault next to his mother. After the burial, the woman was never seen again, nor did they ever discover who she was. All they knew was that she was very private and was reluctant to expose her identity, only going by the name of Miss Le Basi. After Shawn's death, owing much debt, the mansion and property were put up for sale with new owners taking over the run-down estate.

Unfortunately, the new inhabitants of their dream house, purchasing it lock, stock, and barrel for practically a steal, experienced a bit of misfortune. Not long after they settled in, they began to encounter strange and unusual occurrences that were unexplainable and very frightening. Being too afraid to remain in their new home any longer, they decided to pack and move out, swearing that the place was utterly haunted.

Shortly after, the house was once again purchased, this time by a brave and daring couple who found the idea of a haunted house quite exciting. To their dismay, their expectations proved to be far worse than they had anticipated, subjecting them to violent and physical mishaps until the enjoyment of a haunted house was no longer appealing to them.

One night in desperation, the couple deeply concerned for their lives ran out of the house in sheer horror, never again to return. This, of course, placed the estate on the market for a third time and gave credence to the fact that the house was explicitly haunted. As of that day, no one had the courage or interest to purchase a house with such a reputation, believing that Isabel's spirit still lurked in the shadows, cursing and damning anyone who dared to defy her by living in her home.

Beaming with intrigue, Margaret was engrossed by the brief discussion she had with Grace and thanked her for such an informative story. Grateful to find out the specific directions to the Laughton Estate, Margaret, exhausted from her long day's journey, took up lodging at the inn and decided to relax the rest of the day before making a fresh start in the morning.

Up at the crack of dawn, Margaret rose to a radiant morning, and feeling cheerful about her day, she could not wait to begin her investigation. Having a quick bite to eat for breakfast, Margaret, in a rush, shot up from her chair and dashed for the door. In her haste, she caught sight of an incoming man who paused for a moment to light his pipe. Conveying a good morning to the gentleman, she breezed passed him, practically knocking him aside as she darted for her car.

Before she could begin her journey, she first had to stop at the real estate office to acquire access into the house. Taking the short drive to the end of town, she entered the real estate office to find the realtor reading the paper and having his coffee at his desk.

At first impression, the agent mistook her to be a potential buyer once she made inquiries about the Laughton Estate. Not wasting a moment, he rattled off like a chirping bird, elaborating that the twenty-room mansion, sitting on eight hundred seventy-seven acres of land, was a super deal for the money and was just recently reduced for a quick sale, falling short with the history of the house being twice resold due to its haunting inhabitant.

Explaining to the confused man that it was not the reason why she had come, she presented her credentials to the agent, setting the record straight that she was an investigative reporter interested in doing a story on the Laughton Estate. His face flushed, he groaned with disappointment, stating he had no authority to give her access to the property if those were her reasons. However, he did suggest that she contact the Hanes couple and request permission since they lived in Colchester just a few minutes away.

Taking his advice, Margaret, with enthusiasm for her pet project, followed the directions given to her by the realtor and soon arrived at the house of John and Edith Hanes. Parking her car on the circular driveway, she walked the remainder of the cobblestone path, admiring the stone cottage beautifully set on the grassy slope of the hillside. Ringing the doorbell, it was not long before an elderly woman responded, dressed in a dust apron and wearing a smile, candidly asking, "May I help you?"

Inquiring if this was the Hanes residence, Margaret, receiving an affirmative answer, politely introduced herself and informed the woman as to why she had come. Loving to chat, Edith, impressed by Margaret's charm and seeing she was such a sweet young lady, invited her into the house to further discuss the matter. Placing her feather duster down on a nearby chair, Edith led Margaret into the drawing room and offered her a seat on the sofa. Her face brightened, enjoying her company.

Edith liked Margaret from the very start of their discussion; as a journalist, Margaret had mastered pronunciation with such clarity and had such a mild way of expressing herself that it was a pleasure just to listen to her speak. Very comfortable around Margaret, Edith wasted no time, wanting to talk extensively about the estate and the awful ordeals she and her husband had experienced.

"Moving from the big city of Liverpool to a small town of

Colchester to enjoy the tranquility of the countryside was a major decision. At the first sight of our new home, we fell instantly in love with the house, and being such an affordable price, it was a steal, having far more land than we had anticipated. The real estate man was frank, explaining a little of the home's history and informed us of its hauntings. This we accepted, believing the whole idea of having our own personal ghost was exciting. Not long after we moved in and settled down with the exhausting chores of unpacking, we soon began to have our own doubts. For within the first two weeks that elapsed, not a single haunting occurred and we began to wonder, feeling that the ghostly stories were nothing more than a fabrication. We felt we had been misled, and it was all part of the agent's strategy, using this selling pitch, once he saw we were interested in a haunted house. But after all, things could have been worse, and we were lucky enough to have a house we were happy with and at a very affordable price."

She continued, "One evening after a delightful dinner, my husband went to the library as he often did where he preferred to spend some time to relax and indulge himself with his favorite drink. Suddenly while having his drink, a book fell off the shelf and dropped to the floor. Getting up, he thought nothing of the incident. Picking it up, he placed the book back, feeling we had a rodent problem. While resuming his reading and enjoying his brandy, it happened again but this time from the opposite side of the room. Placing the book back, he felt this rodent to be a real nuisance and decided he would hire an exterminator immediately to solve the problem. Once again, he returned to the silence of his reading, and it wasn't long before two books fell and slammed to the floor. Disturbing his peace, he jumped; stunned, his eyebrows shot up with surprise. He felt this was quite extraordinary since the incidents occurred at both sides and exactly at the same time.

"After that day a pattern developed, and he avoided the library altogether, hoping that things would settle down. After a week, he decided to check on the library once again, and as he opened the door, his eyes stood transfixed with shock. He found every book in the library thrown and scattered about the floor. From that day on, we no longer had doubts and became firm believers, convinced that the house was indeed haunted. At first, it seemed that the spirit was taunting us. With the passage of time, the encounters broadened, and the episodes escalated from one mishap to another where physical harm was soon inflicted. This apparently was only the beginning of many more casualties that were to occur."

Looking up from her notepad on which she was feverishly writing, Margaret begged Edith to continue.

Not needing much prompting, Edith picked up from where she left off. "During the evening, my husband now spent his time in the den, rather than the library. I would go to the parlor to relax where I often fell asleep from the comfort of a warm and radiant fire. At times, I would be awakened from a very cold draft coming from the corner of the room and could hear a low voice of a woman weeping. The sobbing would always occur during the night while I sat in the dark with the fire being the only light emanating in the room. The crying gave me such an eerie feeling, running chills up and down my spine, that I would freeze, too afraid to even move an inch, looking into the darkness with haunted eyes. The draft was so cold and intense that it felt as if the front door had been left open in a mid winter blizzard. Frightened to death, I avoided the parlor at night, just as my husband avoided the library.

"Unfortunately, it did not stop there," Edith paused for a moment to take a breath. "My husband, getting more familiarized with the house, walked up to a room in the attic that had glass doors, which led onto a terrace. This room was empty except for an armchair that faced the beautiful view that overlooked the countryside. It appeared to him to be a private place where one could be alone to meditate or collect his thoughts. As he stood by the doors gazing out, he suddenly heard the flapping of wings of some creature in flight. Thinking it was a bird that had trapped itself, he turned to look and flinched, becoming petrified as he spotted a bat. With darting eyes, he followed the bat's every move, becoming alarmed as more bats soon joined in the frenzy. He had no concept where they were coming from. All he knew was that they were flying wildly, and he shifted his body left to right, trying desperately to avoid contact. Before he knew it, the one bat suddenly had become a hundred, and he could feel the swell of panic overwhelm him. To his greatest fear, one bat swooped down so close that it caused him to jump back and fall over the armchair. Now on his hands and knees, he crawled, making his way across the room to the doorway. Taking hold of the doorknob, he stood on his knees and attempted to turn the knob, but somehow the door would not open. The more he tried, the harder it became, and yet he knew the door was not locked or jammed. It felt as if someone was holding it closed from the other side, forbidding his escape. With one mighty tug, it finally opened, and he dived out of the room and onto the hall floor with the door slamming closed behind him. Then the door squeaked as it slowly opened, injecting fear that the bats would follow. As he stood paralyzed, plummeted in horror, he was amazed to find silence and all the bats suddenly disappeared. With luck on his side, he had not been nicked or bitten. Rising to his feet, he descended the steps, and when midway, he was pushed from behind, severely twisting his ankle as he toppled down the stairs. That was the first physical encounter, and my husband suffered for some time before making a complete recovery."

"Oh, my God," cried Margaret, sympathetically. "Mice, bats, noises in the night, and you still stayed in that house?"

"Yes, we did. But there's more. Plenty more," Edith confessed. "The holidays were soon upon us. Since the weather had changed early that year, becoming bitterly cold, having the benefit of a large fireplace in the master bedroom was most appreciated, especially on those cold winter nights. Unfortunately, a fire never lasts forever, and one has to feed it to keep the desired warmth. That is fine while you are awake but while you sleep, it eventually dies out, making the room utterly cold. Apparently neither one of us was willing to leave the warmth of our blankets and bear the chill to maintain the fire, and due to that, our nights were extremely cold. Of course, it started out comfortably warm at first, but during the night I would awaken, feeling frozen, to find the double hinged windows wide open. Jumping up with frost breath, I would race toward the windows and quickly close them, locking the latches. Resuming with my sleep, an hour and a half later I would awaken again, shivering to my bones, again finding the windows wide open, and having to repeat the same process. For four nights, this problem persisted at least twice a night, which became quite disturbing. My husband even checked the latches to see if the locks did indeed hold, and sure enough, they did. There was nothing wrong with the latches or locks, and my husband blamed me for not properly locking them, feeling I was half-asleep. I assured him that was not the case, and to prove it to him, I took extreme measures by tying the latches together securely with rope, making them virtually impossible to open. I was confident that they would not be opened this time. After being awakened at the stroke of two by my mantle clock, I looked up and saw that the windows were still securely closed. Feeling a bit of relief, I resumed with my sleep, and around a quarter to four, once again the room was ice cold with both windows opened wide."

"It was the witch, right?" Margaret chimed in.

"I never swear, but that night, I did," admitted Edith. "Jumping up angrily, I dashed barefoot across the room to those damned windows. Finding the rope untied and left at the windowsill, I stretched out and took hold of each window with my hands, pulling them inward to close them, but somehow this time the metal frames must have jammed or froze, and the windows would not budge an inch. I was struggling vigorously when all of a sudden something grabbed both of my wrists and tried to pull me out the window. If it had not been for the center frame of the double-hinged windows, I would have been pulled clear out of the second floor window and fallen to my death. It felt like a pair of hands holding me tightly that would not let go. To this day, I think of the experience and the close encounter I had with death that night, surviving with only a black eye from hitting the center frame. From that day on, we no longer slept in the master bedroom and used the guest room where the occurrences seemed to cease."

The tone of her voice very serious now, Edith went on, "I got the impression that Isabel wanted to run us out of the house. At that point, I was willing to leave and tried to convince my husband that for our sakes, we should. Apparently, he felt differently, and being a firm man, no ghost was going to run him out of his home. Nevertheless, we did remain, and with the Christmas holidays upon us, we decided to spend it alone and have a quiet evening together listening to our favorite

Christmas carols."

Pausing for a moment while Margaret went into her attaché case for another sharpened pencil, Edith offered to get them some refreshments, but Margaret, so engrossed in the story, declined the offer and asked Edith to instead continue with the account.

Obliging, she began, "Miles, our butler, was also a wonderful cook, and he slaved countless hours preparing a special dinner for us. After our soup, we exchanged our gifts. John gave me a beautiful pearl necklace with matching earrings. I, in turn, gave him a diamond tiepin. Just then, Miles entered with the main course, and the smell of the roasted goose made our mouths water. He was proud of himself for having prepared such a superb treat, decorating the goose with all the trimmings, and his expression reflected his achievement. Crossing from behind John and turning to the side of the table, Miles and the goose crashed to the floor, splattering the entire dinner all over. Shocked, I could not believe what I had just seen. He flew past me as if he had been thrown. Poor Miles, I could still see his face as he looked up at me with the most pitiful eyes, trying to explain that it was not his fault and that he had been pushed very hard from behind. Excited, my husband blew into a rage, raising his fists in defiance, swearing to Isabel that she would never get the best of him."

"That was a brave thing to do," commented Margaret.

"I was clearly shaken and became more frightened by the minute, not knowing what to expect next. I tried to calm my husband down, knowing of his high blood pressure, by trying to put a spin on the disaster. Although the dinner was lost, we could still have our tea and pudding, perhaps save the night, and cheer ourselves by listening to our favorite Christmas songs. Having a smile across his face, my husband was in full agreement to not make this incident get the best of us. After tea, we relaxed in the living room as planned. My husband's spirits seemed to recover, and he began to whistle his favorite Christmas tune while he looked for that particular record. After making his selection and putting on the phonograph, he removed the record from its sleeve. With gaping popped eyes, he recoiled in disbelief once he discovered that his favorite record was broken in two." Standing to make her point,

Edith demonstrated, "Angrily, he tossed it to the floor, quickly fetching another one, only to find that, too, was broken as well. Growing more excited, he grabbed another and then another; upon further inspection, he found all of his records had been destroyed. For the remainder of the night, my husband, deeply saddened, was not at all himself, and I believe that if I were not there, he would have cried. Before retiring that night, I again brought up the subject of leaving. I made my reservations known that under no circumstances would I remain any longer in that house. Looking up in disgust, he said not a word nor gave the slightest argument. By not saying anything at all, he gave me the indication that the possibility was very likely."

"So that's when you put the house back on the market?" questioned Margaret.

"No. Not yet. The following morning at the stroke of eight we proceeded into the dining room as we always did, taking our usual places. Usually Miles would make his entrance, looking cheerful, as he relayed a good morning wish to us as he served breakfast. Unfortunately, that morning that was not at all the case. Sitting there for a good fifteen minutes, we began to speculate as to what had happened to him, and my husband, being a bit edgy, rose from his chair to investigate. I suggested to him that he be patient and give Miles an extra few minutes, thinking he might be busy, but by half past eight, my husband refused to wait another minute and jumped up from his seat and headed for the kitchen to find out what was causing the delay. To his surprise, he discovered that breakfast had not been prepared, and Miles was nowhere in sight. After informing me of the irregularities, he felt perhaps that Miles may have become ill during the night, and so he decided to check on him in his room. After a few short minutes, he returned looking puzzled since Miles was not in his room nor had his bed been slept in. Becoming worried and just to make sure Miles had not seriously injured himself or was rendered unconscious, he made a quick check throughout the house and basement. Still, Miles was nowhere to be found. Reaching another probable cause, he felt Miles was short on food and may have taken the car into town for some provisions. Darting out the door to the garage, he was surprised even further to find the car still there and in the very same place he had parked it. Reflecting on a passing thought, he began to wonder what could have happened. With the events unfolding, his disappearance was becoming more and more of a mystery. Being so frustrated, it had not crossed his mind until now that there could be one other possibility to explain his disappearance. Having his own private phone in his room, Miles could have received an important call during the night. With such an emergency and time being crucial, he would have had to leave at the spur of the moment and probably did not want to disturb us from our sleep. Although my husband found it strange that he did not leave a note, he would give him the benefit of the doubt. If Miles did not contact us within a day or two, he would then notify the police and file a missing person's report."

"So what happened to Miles?" Margaret impatiently asked. Edith's chronicle of events were so vivid, Margaret felt like she knew him.

"For the rest of the day, our labors and chores were many, and we wondered how Miles ever managed to do all the work on his own. Not having the cooking techniques with which Miles was gifted, breakfast and dinner turned out to be total disasters. Forcing down a charred roast, we grimaced to overly strong coffee. It felt strange not to see Miles there. After all, having been in our employ for the last thirteen years, he had become very dear to us, and we were very grateful when he had agreed to make the move along with us. After our day, we retired early, being very exhausted. Sitting up relaxing in bed, my husband, who was reading a book, turned to me and implored me to reconsider my feelings about leaving. Stressing that he did love the house, having plenty of land gave him a certain feeling of privacy and freedom. I looked at him as one wanting to stomp on a bug. Taunted and filled with disgust, I had never felt more crazed in my entire life. 'I will not hear of this,' I screamed at him, hitting my fist on the mattress, and then shutting my light, I angrily turned over on my side. Apparently, he knew I was very distressed, and soon after, he said not a word, closed his light, and went to sleep."

Stopping only momentarily to reposition herself in her chair, Edith began again. "Around one in the morning, my eyes popped open, thinking I smelled smoke. Sitting up in bed, I sniffed the air again to confirm my worst fears. Good God, I thought, my suspicions were right, and jumping to my feet, I dashed for the door. Taking hold of the doorknob, I flung it wide open and stood transfixed with horror. There before my very eyes, flames engulfed the entire stairwell, crackling embers and timbers falling; the whole room was filled with smoke. Panic-stricken, a lump pocketed in my throat, and I was unable to warn my husband. Still sound asleep, he did not know the house was ablaze. With one more effort, I let out a blood-curdling scream, this time alarming my husband. Awakened by my cries, his eyes peered widely about, still feeling groggy and wondering what was causing all the excitement. 'Get up you fool,' I shouted. 'The whole place is on fire.' Running out of the bedroom, we escaped safely using the rear staircase. With the flames spreading so rapidly, we did not have time to call the fire department. Instead, we raced for the garage, took the car, and drove the ten minutes into town where we alerted them."

"How frightening," Margaret said, her voice showing genuine concern.

"I had never been that scared before in my life," Edith responded. "My whole body was shaking. Handing us blankets to shield us from the cold, we remained in the firehouse while the detail set off to fight the fire. In half an hour, the fire trucks returned, and I thought to myself how remarkable and experienced they were to put out a fire so quickly. Just then, the fire chief approached us, looking quizzical, inquiring if we had been drinking. Stating we hadn't, I questioned why he asked. To our surprise, his answer came to us as a sudden shock, once he informed us that the house had not been on fire at all. Feeling agitated from the accusations, I snapped back, feeling my face flushed as I bellowed, 'That is impossible. I saw it—the whole damn place was on fire!' Rolling his eyes back in annoyance, I could see he was growing impatient with us. He angrily demanded we leave the station house, stating he and his men had more important things to do than run around to false alarms. In all my life, I have never felt as humiliated as I did that night."

"No fire? I don't understand. What exactly happened then?" Margaret questioned.

"As it was, the fire chief was quite right. There was no fire or damage sustained to the house. Isabel had created an illusion so convincing that it fooled all our senses. I still can't believe it. It was tangible, so real. After smelling the smoke, seeing the flames, feeling the heat, and hearing the crackling of embers, it turned out to be nothing more than our mere imaginations. From that day on, I refused to live in that house or set foot in it, even for a split second, fearful of not knowing what to believe. My husband was inclined to agree with me, and without any squabbling this time, we put the house up for sale. We felt no house, no matter how great it was, was worth our lives. It may have taken some adjusting to get used to a smaller house with far less land, but emphasizing the point, it is far more important to live unafraid, happy, and with peace of mind."

"Did Miles ever return?"

"No," Edith sighed heavily. "Deeply concerned for Miles, my husband contacted some known relatives whose number we had in the event of an emergency. Apparently, they as well had not heard from him, and we informed them that we had already filed a disappearance report with the police. Until today, we still have never found out what exactly happened to him. I miss him and think of him quite frequently. I have my own suspicions, believing that it was Isabel and that cursed house that drove him off into madness, but my husband, not being as imaginative as I am, felt my way of thinking was a bit eccentric."

"So there you have it! The entire account of each occurrence we experienced in that wicked house. It was never my intention to frighten you, and I hope I haven't, but I do caution you upon your visit to take extreme care," Edith warned, pointing her finger in the air for effect.

At that particular moment, she caught sight of a little skepticism in Margaret's face. Wanting to make sure Margaret understood the seriousness of the situation, Edith cautioned, "I too once felt that way when the realtor informed me that the house was haunted. Nevertheless, after experiencing each encounter that soon became worse than the previous mishap, my outlook suddenly changed, and I became totally afraid."

Being the sweet, gentle lady that Edith was, she lent Margaret her own personal keys to the estate. Bidding each other goodbye with warm smiles, Margaret thanked Edith once again for such an inspiring story. Escorting her to the door, Edith, who sensed Margaret might blindly throw caution to the wind, made one thing clear, assuring her that everything she had explained to her was the truth and was not at all a fabrication to impress her. Fondly, she wished her good luck on her assignment and surprised her with an affectionate embrace, remaining at the door until Margaret got into her car and drove away.

******

With morning now well past into mid afternoon and not wanting to waste the day, Margaret set her sights for the Laughton Estate. On her ride, overwhelmed by the radiant scenery, she admired the rolling hills of the countryside. Covered in foliage, the array of the autumn colors blended into a staggering view for her to behold. That entire splendor took her mind off things, and she did not realize how quickly she arrived at her destination.

It was quite obvious that she had found the right place with its massive mason walls and arched gates that clearly defined in big bold letters, The Laughton Estate, with the family's crest beneath it.

Parking adjacent to the mason walls, her engine still running, Margaret approached the towering gates, unlocked the padlock, and unraveled the oversized chain. With years of rust, the doors strained as they slid apart, screeching so loudly, irritating one's teeth down to the bone. She was able, with all her might, to push aside the heavy gates and make an opening wide enough for her car to pass. Driving through the gateway, she then proceeded to park on the side of the shoulder, deciding to walk the rest of the way, feeling much could be explored on foot.

It would be a half a mile before she reached the mansion. With each approaching step, she gave thought to the extent of Edith's warning. As she turned the bend, her eyes caught sight of a wondrous spectacle, and her thoughts of fear were momentarily put aside. It was radiant and filled with splendor. Never before had she seen an array of trees and shrubs such as these, and she felt as if she was in the midst of a botanical garden, coexisting with nature and its beauty. Upon reaching the apex of the slope, the mansion was clearly visible. Covered in ivy and overshadowed by a westerly sun, it stood there in the emptiness of its solitude.

As Margaret meditated over the horizon, she felt it was a shame for a house as lovely as this with its unique architecture to be uninhabited and not be enjoyed by any family. Then too there was a dark side to this hypothesis that was mysterious, yet very sinister, where evil dwelled in the darkness and consumed to madness anyone who dared to behold its elegance. After taking a wide-angle photograph of the house, she descended the hill and finally made her way to the front door. That feeling of anxiety once again gripped her as she inserted the key, only to find that the door had already been unlocked. Cautiously, she slowly opened the door, and with a spur of wind, several leaves spiraled into the vestibule upon her entry.

Walking to the hall that led to the main stairway, she knew well from Edith's description the arrangement of the house with the parlor left of her, the library on the right, and the sleep chambers on the second floor. With the potential for a high concentration of hauntings, Margaret felt those rooms would be the most interesting and best suited for her photographs.

Walking straight for the dining room where Miles had been completely thrown off his feet, spoiling a delightful Christmas dinner, she removed the white linens that covered the furniture and took an overall shot of the dining room table and chairs. Standing to the side of the table, she took an additional two photos of the location where Miles was believed to have fallen, hitting hard against the breakfront.

Replacing the linens in the dining room, she then made her way to the library. It was an enormous room, she thought as she entered. Filled with books from wall to wall, its literature touched on just about every subject needed for the intellectual mind. It also had a cast, spiral staircase leading to an overhead platform that overshadowed the level below. But the place she found most interesting was the armchair positioned in the center of the room, offset by a pedestal table and a freestanding Tiffany lamp. It was here, in this very spot, that John had witnessed the very first haunting. As Margaret's eyes narrowed speculatively, casting some doubt, she was somewhat disappointed, having not sighted one apparition or disturbance. For that matter, she did not know what to expect, and if a book or two did fly out of the shelves, she would have felt the rush of adrenalin, being ready to catch the action on her rapid shot camera.

With the dining room and library now covered, she decided to photograph the parlor where Edith's restful sleep was disturbed by those ghoulish cries and cold drafts. Venturing into the parlor, this room was to be one of the highlights of her article. To make sure that the atmosphere, mood, and realization were captured, she wanted that armchair and small table with the fireplace in the background all snapped into one picture. Unfortunately, the room was too dark for her lens, and pacing over to the windows, she drew open the draperies, emitting the light to fill the room. She could see it was a cozy room with blue and white wallpaper and wide plank hardwood floors. It also was beautifully arranged with the charm and warmth of solid wood valances and sheer, white curtains, overlapped by draperies that had a soft touch of blue to match the décor of the couch and armchair. Coming around from behind the couch, she set herself in line for the picture of the armchair before the fireplace. Too close, she took a few steps back and raised the camera to her face in order to focus her view of that particular location. Looking through the viewfinder, her face became glazed with shock; bewildered, she saw a woman sitting in the armchair before a blazing fire.

Placing the camera down quickly to reaffirm the image she had just seen, Margaret, spooked by the elusive, idly stared in disbelief, seeing nothing more than the emptiness of the armchair and no fire. Feeling a bit apprehensive, she raised the camera to her eye again, and with suspicion that the appearance would occur, she snapped her picture, this time without the delusion of her imagination.

She felt perhaps she must have been far more nervous than she realized with her mind playing out the thoughts and warnings of Edith's ghost stories. Achieving her desire, she covered the furniture and drew the draperies, leaving the parlor as she had found it.

From the parlor, she entered the hall and ascended the steps to the bedrooms. Walking down the corridor, she opened each door along her way until she found the master bedroom. Entering the spacious room, she was overcome by the beauty of its interior and that large white marble mantle that was positioned in the center of the room. The furniture was very old by today's standards and would be considered very rare antique pieces. Besides a carved-leaf, double-door armoire with a set of drawers on the bottom, there was also a mahogany dresser with folding mirrors, enabling one to view both sides of the face simultaneously. At the right of the dresser stood an oak chest on chest in the corner of the room, and not far from that was a magnificent four-poster tester bed with a canopy frame that was breathtaking.

As Margaret swung around to see behind her, one piece grasped her attention and that was the custom-made curio built into the wall. It wasn't so much the curio itself that deterred her and gave her the creeps; it was the awful items that lay within the shelves that she detested, giving her an uncomfortable feeling. Dolls, lots and lots of those hideous-looking dolls.

It was odd for a girl to feel this way, and although now an adult, that feeling still remained with her to this day. Usually youngsters loved their little teddy bears and dolls and found them to be the most popular choice. While she did not dread every doll she saw, some affected her more than others, especially the old-fashioned types, the ones with porcelain heads, painted hair, and shiny white faces outlined by those red ruby lips.

As a child, she always had a fear of dolls and clowns. In the tour of the circus, you would not find Margaret among the roaring crowd in the stands where the clowns were concerned. While everyone was jumping with joy and laughing hysterically, she stood silent and stiff, turning her face away, diverting her eyes until the act was completed.

To Margaret, dolls were sinister looking; their blank expressions and cold, dead stares gave her the chills. She could recall her days as a child. Her mother once owned two dolls very similar to the ones in the curio and kept them on the rocking chair. As much as Margaret loved to play on that rocker, she would not approach it and have her fun unless her mother removed the dolls first. She could not rightfully explain why she had this great fear; all she knew was that she did, and somehow it must have had a psychological effect on her, probably being her own fault for never facing up to her fears.

Diverting her eyes as she always did when she became upset, she turned her back to the curio and walked to the door. Standing before the open entrance, she wanted to take a wide-angle picture of the bedroom. As she placed the camera to her face and looked through the viewfinder, she was surprised once more as the image of the phantasm appeared again. This time the figure of the woman stood before a freestanding mirror and sneered at Margaret through her reflection. The face was unreal, like that of a painted porcelain doll with a piercing stare and red ruby lips that wickedly grinned at her with pleasure, knowing of her fright. Lowering the camera, Margaret wanted to see if the effigy would go away and sure enough, it did, but the instant she raised the viewfinder to her eye again, the image reappeared, this time mocking her by sticking out a long tongue and laughing at her. She turned sharply to the right as she heard the increase of more laughter. Her face masked with terror, she could see that the dolls in the curio had all joined in on the laughter, looking at her with devilish smiles and cold, stone stares.

Margaret knew that if she remained there for another minute, she would pass out from sheer fright. Without delay, she raced from the room, stirred from the haunting, and with her face flush to the hall wall, she braced for a moment to recover her breath.

Feeling faint, she carefully descended the steps and made her way to the kitchen, desperately needing some water. Wanting to wet her handkerchief, she opened the spindles of the faucet, only to discover that the house water had been shut off. Turning to her right, it was with luck that she saw an old-fashioned hand pump mounted on a platform of a hand dug well. Observing years of rust and decay upon the pump, she prayed that the mechanism was still functional. Supporting her weight against the fixture, she took hold of the handle, cranking it hard to draw water. Not seeing a single drop and feeling extremely thirsty, her endurance won out over her weakness, motivating her to pump once more, this time adding a bit more vigor. As the pump squeaked to the rhythm of her drive, she heard gurgling emitted from the spout. How grotesque, she thought! The smell was so excruciating that one could have vomited on the spot. With her thirst subsided now and replaced by a queasy stomach, she no longer had an eagerness for water but instead preferred a bit of relief from some fresh air.

Covering her nose and mouth with her handkerchief, she gave thought as to what could cause that awful stench. The odor smelled like something rotted, something very dead, and being the inquisitive type, she had to see. Looking down at the platform, she saw a pull handle attached to the trap door of the well. Using a good deal of strength, she forced it free and flipped open the trap door onto its back. It was pitch black as she gazed down, emitting a cold, damp draft with the smell beginning to vent out and quickly fill the kitchen. Removing a flashlight from her coat pocket, she got down on her knees, taking extreme caution not to fall into the large opening. Bent over, she looked down into the pit, probing around curiously with her flashlight. With popped eyes, she gasped, as she stood there riveted in horror. Below her on the bottom of the shallow well was a partly decayed skeleton of a man. Dressed in a butler's outfit, face up, eyes sunken in their sockets, and having a gaping mouth, he seemed to wear the expression of his sheer fright.

Trembling, she was unable to bear any more of this disgusting sight and ran out of the kitchen, heading a straight path for the front door with heart pounding and nerves shattered. Resting herself on the stone step, Margaret began to recover her composure, relaxing and taking in breaths of fresh air. With her mind becoming clear, she now realized where Miles had disappeared. For the moment, she did not want to return into the house and decided she would instead look for the family crypt.

Feeling much better, she continued with her investigation by choosing a different path from the way she had come, and instead of sticking to the road, she took a shortcut across the field. She had no concept of where it was or what sort of structure to expect; all she did know was that she had to cover quite a bit of property in hopes of finding the crypt.

From the open pasture, she began to approach the foot of the forest and noticed a very large willow tree that stood out, giving plenty of shade. As she stepped closer to the tree, she caught sight of the bare bark that had a heart with the initials S and R in it. She felt this to be a private place, and she assumed that Shawn had carved it to show his love for Rachel. Feeling this sentiment would be very appealing to her readers, she decided to take a picture of the heart, showing a love that once was, in a place that was considered to be their castle.

As she removed the camera from her bag, she felt a sadness for the two lovers who were once forbidden and plagued by misfortune, and she hoped that in their after-life they would be happily reunited. Now focusing on the tree, she saw, in the right of the viewfinder, a figure of a woman at a distance. She assumed that the haunting image had reoccurred, and she lowered her camera to look, only to be surprised to find the figure still there. Snapping her picture quickly, she raced the hundred yards up the slope to confront the woman who by now had lowered herself to her knees.

Not having the slightest indication of what she was doing or why she was there, all Margaret could see, as she made her approach, was that the woman was digging beneath the soil using a hand spade. Hearing a hello that shrieked from behind, the old woman jumped, turned sharply, and stood frozen with her eyes blinking excessively. Realizing she had frightened the poor woman half to death, Margaret offered her sincere apology as she quickly introduced herself.

Seeing the basket half filled with mushrooms, Margaret commented on how lucky she was to find all those truffles without the assistance of a pig. She had always been under the impression that the keen sense of a pig was needed to locate the truffles; otherwise, one could dig endlessly and not find a thing. The old woman assured her that there was nothing special about the technique; all that was needed was patience and years of experience with a knack of knowing where to dig.

"Watch for the suillia fly," the old woman suggested, "and just below where she lays her eggs, you can bet truffles will be found nearby."

Smiling, Margaret had a curious yen to know who she was and asked if she was from around the area. Stating her name was Desa, she claimed she lived not far off. Since the season was right, she took the liberty of looking for white truffles by the large oaks, which she had always done for many years without objection.

Feeling Desa's knowledge of the property could be beneficial, Margaret inquired if she knew where the Laughton crypt was located. Happy to accommodate Margaret, Desa retorted, "Of course, I do. It's not very far from where we stand, and if you'd like, I could take you there."

As promised, Desa led the way, and they soon arrived at the family mausoleum. Once inside, it became obvious, upon her first inspection, that the crypt had been used as a place of refuge. Seeing embers simmering in the fireplace, there was evidence of cookware and utensils messily scattered about. She also noticed a high-back fire chair at the side of the fireplace, along with a table that had an empty cup upon it, and a candlestick burnt down midway. Off to her left, just beyond the dimly lit chamber, she could see a pile of straw on the side of the vault and an indentation outlining a body where someone had slept. Being under a gloomy atmosphere such as this, Margaret could not understand why someone would choose to live among the dark, the dampened cold, and the foul odor of the decaying dead.

Finding this out of the ordinary, she questioned Desa, asking if she had noticed any other trespassers on the property. Remarking that she hadn't, she made note that these sorts of things did occur often with squatters making their homes in places that were uninhabited.

Pacing closer to the straw pile, Margaret looked down at the crypt and saw that the vault was Shawn's resting place. She was mystified when she discovered that several children's storybooks were left on top of the vault and droppings of melted candle wax could be seen scattered about. She was also astounded to see that fresh flowers had been placed there as well, neatly contained in a small vase filled with water. For the life of her, she could not figure out who could have left them, and still standing with her back to Desa, she commented, making her detection verbally known.

Receiving no reply, she turned sharply, soon realizing the reason for Desa's lack of response. Not finding her there any longer, she just assumed she had continued with her mushroom hunting.

Being inquisitive, Margaret's nose for journalism itched to further investigate her mysterious surroundings. Looking at the crypt next to Shawn's, she distinctly noted from the date on Isabel's tomb the peculiarity of a lack of information. It was unusual, she thought, that dates for events as important as these were incomplete; the description of the birth was clearly marked, but the date of death was not. How strange this was, she pensively thought. What could have been the reason for this slip up?

As she pondered further, she felt there could have been one of many reasons for this blunder. It was very feasible that there might not have been any family members left to assume charge of the funeral and see whether all the arrangements were properly met by the undertaker. Nevertheless, she was not greatly concerned, and she brushed it off as a professional oversight of one who was very sloppy in the performance of his work.

Walking back toward the fireplace to the table, Margaret picked up the cup and saucer, and after closely examining them, she took note that the china was rather expensive. Only seeing the back of the chair upon her entry, she had not noticed until now that a comb and hand mirror were left on the seat. Once again, she found those personal articles quite striking as she saw that the set was made of pure silver, far beyond the means of any ordinary squatter. Apparently, whoever owned them surely had a taste for elegance and must have at one time had money in order to afford such lavish items. Yet as an afterthought, she supposed she might have misconstrued the matter and possibly made it out to be more than it actually was, where the simple fact was nothing more than a thief possessing stolen goods.

With morning gone, having had her fill of the puzzling work of a detective, Margaret decided to do what she had come for in the first place. Attaching a flash to her camera, she photographed the interior of the chamber from different points, and having three remaining frames, she took Isabel's and Shawn's vaults, saving the last frame for the crypt's entrance.

Once outside, before returning to town, she used her final shot, taking an overall picture of the entrance leading down to the family's vault. She hoped on her way back that she would again meet up with Desa, having many curious questions to ask her. As Margaret walked back to her car, she took the same path that led to the large oak trees, having a hunch she would find Desa somewhere along the way. However, to her dismay, Desa was nowhere to be sighted, and she secured the gates, looking back toward the horizon just before she departed.

She was actually excited that during her short stay at the Laughton Estate, she had already uncovered many interesting discoveries. Besides solving Miles' strange disappearance by finding him in the well, there was also the flaw on Isabel's tomb, the flowers, and the family crypt, which was used as a place of refuge. However, the one thing that kept popping into her mind was Desa.

She couldn't put her finger on it as yet, but it troubled her for some unknown reason of which she was unable to explain. She felt Desa knew more than she revealed, and she even had a hunch that she might have been that squatter herself. There was something uncanny about her, and she noted that Desa had a way about her that seemed sure, free, and unafraid, which struck Margaret to be peculiar characteristics for someone who was a trespasser. It was evident that when they first met, Desa did not seem to be the least bit frightened or worried, not in the sense of being startled but of being caught as a trespasser. After all, the offense was quite serious, and an offender could spend several months behind bars.

While she gave serious thought to the surrounding circumstances, she realized she was probably being a bit too harsh on Desa and could see that her journalistic instincts were again getting the best of her. Although she was indecisive at times, as she drove back to town, she abandoned her theory and believed that it was probably nothing at all.

By now, she felt completely sympathetic toward Desa, and even though she was a squatter, she felt she could at least show her some compassion, knowing she was an old woman who was homeless and who had nowhere else to live. After all, why should she be a villain and report her to the police, making the poor woman suffer more than she already had?

Parking her car at the curb in front of the inn, she decided not to disclose that one detail, feeling she was making the right decision by not exposing Desa's existence to the police as an inhabitant of the Laughton family's crypt.

Chapter XXIII

The Discovery

That evening while having a quiet, enjoyable dinner, Grace surprisingly approached Margaret. Looking bright-eyed and having a curious yen, she sat alongside of Margaret as she inquired how her day had gone at the Laughton Estate. Cautiously looking around the room, Margaret huddled closer to Grace, and in a whisper, she relayed in detail her excursions at the manor.

She was captivated, strung with suspense, as she stood there with eyes wide, while Margaret disclosed her day from start to finish, ending with the climactic murder scene of Miles.

"You must report this immediately," Grace muttered.

"I have already done so. Earlier today, I consulted with Sergeant Striker and reported the discovery, and he assured me that he would see to it straight away."

Yet the thrill of the mood still gripped Grace, and she wanted to know whom the person was that she had met on the property and how she looked. With the sighting revealed, Margaret conveyed her early morning encounter with the woman on a hillside who hunted for truffles by the large oak trees. "This woman claimed she lived a short distance from the Laughton Estate and sort of had the right to pick mushrooms on the property. She seemed very intelligent and able to comprehend everything. She must have known Isabel since she made it a point to tell me that she thought Isabel was a righteous person who was persecuted unfairly for raising and defending a bastard as her own."

"What did she look like?" Grace interrupted, sounding like a small child engrossed in a story.

"Well, her posture was hunched slightly, and she walked with a pronounced limp, supporting herself with the use of a long stick cane. She was rather old looking, haggard, and untidy, with long white hair tied back in a French braid."

Margaret, still not finished with her description, was again interrupted by Grace. "Did she tell you her name?"

"Yes," Margaret laughed at Grace's excited tone. "She called herself Desa."

At that moment, Grace's expression completely changed, and with a dropped jaw and eyes wide, she froze as if she had seen a ghost. At that instant, it became obvious to Margaret that something was terribly wrong. "What is it?" she curiously asked as she saw the sudden fright on Grace's face.

"I believe you met the witch," Grace hinted with a quiver in her voice. "By your description it is evident that it was Isabel. From the mere fact of that name to the distinct hairdo, I am fully convinced it had to be her. Somehow I never mentioned this to anyone, feeling sympathetic and respectful of their intimacy by not exposing this one detail of their private lives, but after hearing that name uttered, it made me aware of the obscure truth. The name is not common nor one with which anyone is well familiar. Being original, it was solely created from the lips of a child before his age of understanding. In the early days of his childhood, Desa was the name Shawn used to call his mother. So you can understand why I was suddenly shocked once you told me this."

"But how could this be possible?" Margaret blinked with surprise. "If that was Isabel I met, she would have been at least one hundred twenty-five years old by now, and this person certainly did not look like any corpse to me."

With a glance, Grace could see that Margaret's face was glazed with shock, and showing concern, she tried her best to make her understand the different varieties of witches and the powers they possessed. "Like my customers, you are unaware that there are many kinds of witches."

"Many kinds of witches? I thought a witch was a witch," Margaret admitted, taking another sip of her tea.

"You're thinking of the typical witch portrayed on Halloween who had a wart tipped nose, owned a black cat, and flew on a broomstick at the stroke of midnight."

With a glowing look, Margaret's face lit up like a little child mesmerized and gripped by fascination. "Tell me about the witches. It'll be good for my article."

"I see I got your interest. There's the soothsayer, the juggler, incantatory, venefice, and the white witch, better known as the good witch."

"There's a good witch? Wait. Let me write this all down," said Margaret, intrigued, taking a pad and pencil out from her attaché case.

"Yes, unfortunately, despite her skills and good intentions of curing both animal and man, she turned out to be the most persecuted of all the witches. Unlike the good witch, Isabel's mother had a dark side and was known as a venefice."

"What does that mean? I don't understand."

"She's the poisoner, and you know what happened to the four maids who were under her employment. Whatever she used to poison them, apparently it was a good substance. So good that it was undetectable in a lab, and despite the authorities' suspicions, she was never prosecuted for a single murder. She was quite clever. In each incident, she covered up the death to make it appear as an accident or illness, blaming the death on fever or heart failure from hard work. As a matter of fact, in one case the deceased was found on the bottom of the staircase. Isabel's mother claimed she had heard a loud crash and a solid thumping during the evening. Racing out of her bedroom, she discovered the maid dead with her eyes wide and her face masked with terror. It was strange because no one else in the household heard the crash. Even though

Isabel's father was across the hall, directly in front of the staircase, he did not hear a sound. But what was even more extraordinary was the doctor who examined her at the scene. According to the circumstances, he found her death to be most peculiar, considering she fell down a marble staircase, and not one bruise or broken bone was found on her body."

"They were never able to prove her guilt?" Margaret questioned as she fiddled with her pencil.

"No, never!" said Grace, shaking her head. "Right up until the day she died, the authorities were unable to prove not one murder. But let's get back to the witches and Isabel. Isabel was gifted in her craft. As an incantatory, her powers were wide and broad. You already know some of the things she was capable of—casting spells, embodiment by placing herself in a desired creature, creating phantasms. But the one thing she could not do was raise the dead."

"She would have definitely used that to bring Shawn back to life."

"Right, but she could prolong life and remain healthy until the very end. Isabel crossed the lines and possessed certain powers of other witches, and being truly unique, she was feared for her supremacy."

"How could that be?"

"Who knows? But she exceeded her powers and seemed to be many types of witches all rolled into one. She's not one to mess with! Be careful, Margaret!"

"Oh, don't worry about me," Margaret said confidently. "I'm quite capable of taking care of myself."

Grace was just about to answer when she noticed that the dining room was now full and she had to run to assist with the demands of the customers. Jumping from her chair, she apologized for having to dash off, explaining they would speak again later.

******

Margaret, who had already finished eating dinner, decided to return to her room. She was exhausted from the long day's activity at the Laughton Estate and wanted nothing more than to take a bath and sink into a soft mattress.

Although her body ached for sleep, her mind was fully conscious, feeling unrest from her recent conversation with Grace. She was mystified by Grace's implications about Desa and whether or not this person was indeed Isabel. She did find it hard to believe that after one hundred and twenty-five years, Isabel could still be alive and well, seeking refuge under an assumed name and eluding the public by faking her death.

As Margaret thought about Desa, many things crossed her mind that could substantiate Grace's extraordinary claim. From her first meeting with Desa to the moment she cast eyes on the crypt, she found the scenario to be very possible. As she lie awake reviewing her day, she tried to piece together the facts, giving a better prospective to the overall picture. From what she gathered, the crypt, comb, mirror, children's storybooks, and fresh flowers on Shawn's grave were suspicious.

Besides fitting the description and the use of the name Desa that gave birth and rise to this sudden revelation, there was also another thing that she found extremely odd. When Desa thought Margaret wasn't looking, she tossed a log onto the simmering fire to keep it burning. She never mentioned it to Desa, yet she did find this action to be a bit peculiar. For the mere fact that although it was virtually impossible for the wood to be seen in the obscurity of the darkened corner, it appeared that Desa knew exactly where the wood was and went right to it without the slightest hesitation. It was apparent that for a person who had no affiliation with the place, she knew well where things were. After giving it considerable thought, it all made sense, and she felt she had stumbled on a breakthrough that disputed medical science.

How remarkable it was, she thought. She could see it all as she lay in bed, the living proof of an existing witch who had lived to be one hundred twenty-five years old. It would be the discovery of the century. She would gain fame and fortune, and her name would be plastered all over newspapers and magazines. This, in turn, would open doors and pave the way for opportunities on radio, guest appearances on talk shows, and she might possibly even win an award for the best journalist of the year. Yet all her fame and fortune could not come about unless she knew the truth and had proof to back it up, such as photographs and possibly even a taped interview with Isabel herself.

Feeling time was wasting, she leapt out of bed and refilled her camera with a fresh roll of film. This was one scoop she certainly wasn't going to lose by forgetting something she desperately needed. "Batteries, flashbulbs, extra film, tape recorder, flashlight," she could be heard muttering as she gave note to the remembrance of each item. As she took precautions, she made it a point not to forget anything by double-checking once more before placing each item into her photo bag.

Taking a quick glance at her wristwatch, at half past eight the night was young, and she felt she had everything she needed for tonight's objective. Hastily, she dashed out of her room and raced down the steps, cutting a path through the densely filled dining room, exiting the door. With the weekend crowd, the inn was filled to capacity, and with so much activity, pleasure, and games to attract one's attention, no one even noticed that she left.

Once outside, she paused, giving final thought to her equipment, and confident she had it all, she tossed the bag onto the front seat, starting her car. As she drove to the edge of town, she distinctly noticed the loss of adequate light. It was apparent that the street lamps by the storefronts that brightly lit the town soon became a pall of sheer darkness. With nothing to see except the road before her, Margaret felt a little apprehensive and drove much slower than her usual speed, taking some extra caution. It was for reasons such as these, she very rarely drove at night, for she feared breaking down, poor visibility, or becoming disoriented after losing her bearings.

Glancing back through her rear-view mirror, she could see the glimmer of lights slowly fading away. Apparently, what had been virtually clear and recognizable during the day did not hold true at night, impairing her sense of direction and giving her doubts as to whether she would ever find the Laughton Estate.

Despite Margaret's qualms, she could not afford to lose this opportunity, and determined as she was, she pressed on, prevailing over her anxieties. With a drive that should have been no more than a fifteen-minute commute, Margaret was on the road for more than half an hour and believed she had lost her way. Overwhelmed, she did not have the slightest indication of where she was.

Consumed with disgust, she realized her anxiousness may have been a mistake, and she felt it best to continue her search in the morning. With the road so narrow, she was forced to drive until she could find a location wide enough to permit her to turn. As luck would have it, it was then as she cut the sharp bend that her headlights flashed across the gates, revealing her destination. She was reprieved and felt relief as she swerved over to nose her car up to the gates. Feeling her car was safely off the road, Margaret, still having possession of the keys, unfastened the lock, and giving the gate a slight push to one side, she was able to slip through the narrow space.

Although it was pitch black and hard to see at night, Margaret knew that if she kept to the pavement it would eventually lead her to the manor. Taking out her trusted flashlight, she followed the road under the haze of fog, and with a bit of bad luck that made matters worse, it began to rain.

By the time she reached the house, she was drenched to the bone. Feeling cold and wet, she stepped under the carriage drive to get out of the rain that poured down in buckets. Being so worried about forgetting something for tonight's objectives, she laughed at herself for failing to bring an umbrella. Removing her handkerchief from her coat pocket, she dried her face and then proceeded to walk to the vestibule's entrance where she found the door wide open as she had left it.

In the cover of the night, everything seemed so creepy and eerie, and she felt the darkness had taken control. As she lingered at the doorway, she probed with her flashlight before she entered the room. With each step, fear of the intangible heightened, and in a conscious effort, she tried to protect herself from the unspeakable. Once inside, she could clearly see the glare of the moon rays that pierced through the windows, and her imagination and visions took on a hidden meaning. She didn't know why she felt as jumpy as she did. Perhaps the night, not being able to see, and not knowing what to expect made all the difference. Suddenly, she heard a noise and then footsteps thereafter.

She turned her ear to listen intently and became aware that someone was in the house as well. Instantly, she dashed off and wedged her body next to the vestibule mirror. Feeling concealed in the darkened corner, she watched quietly as an intruder approached. Out of the shadows, a lit candle first appeared, and she recognized the woman to be Isabel, carrying some extra needed candles tucked away under her arm. From the hall, she entered the parlor, and it was not long before she heard a click and a solid thump. By the time she reached the parlor to investigate, Isabel was nowhere in the room to be found. What had happened to her? Where could she have possibly gone? Standing motionless and looking dumbfounded, she contemplated the mysterious disappearance.

Then it suddenly hit her and she remembered. According to Inspector Gibbs' story, Dutch had been using a secret passageway that led from the parlor to the family's crypt. Ahh, that's where she had gone, she suspiciously reflected, shaking her head.

Eager to know where the passageway was hidden, she felt its discovery would prove interesting to her readers. Keenly surveying the interior by eye, she eliminated the parts of the room that would not be suitable to conceal a secret tunnel. She immediately dismissed the partition on the left, noting there were three large windows spread out across the wall. Her second elimination came just as quickly as she stood by the entrance and saw that the wall was too narrow to house a trap door with a room just on the other side of it. It all boiled down to two remaining walls, the one straight ahead where the fireplace and bookshelves were or the wall off to her right.

Compelled by an uncontrollable eagerness, she turned to her right and began her search on the oak paneled wall. Flashing the light carefully across the surface, she scrutinized just about every inch, seeking some sort of button, latch, or pull ring that would release a door trap. With fatigue setting in after over an hour of a tiresome search that seemed to be going nowhere, her intuition assured her that the passageway just was not there.

With a change of plans, she turned her sights to the fireplace wall. Her inclination this time made her feel more confident, convinced that the passageway had to be hidden somewhere within the obscurity of the bookshelves. Going with her suspicions, she concentrated on the fireplace inlay, pushing, feeling, and pulling every emboss in hopes of activating a door. After some time and still not finding anything of significance, she paused to catch her breath before flashing her light on the bookshelf she decided to proceed to next.

The task seemed tedious and laborious, but determined as she was, she would not give in to failure. There she was deep into it again, with her nose probing the bookshelf left of the fireplace. Unsuccessful, she had misgivings, but still she pressed on and expanded her wearisome search to the other side, hyped by the hope of that one discovery.

Unfortunately and to her dismay, despite spending a great deal of effort and time and combing through the shelves thoroughly, she came up empty handed. Dissatisfied and feeling weary, she knew that the switch was hidden somewhere within, but she just had not been lucky enough to stumble across it as of yet.

Though most people would have given up by then, Margaret, stubborn as she was, did not accept defeat willingly. As a journalist, she was taught to pursue her objectives, especially when her instincts made her feel certain of the prospect. Giving it one final go, she decided to remove all the books from the shelves to look behind them in hopes of finding that damn switch. This way she would have no doubt in her mind that she had covered every possibility.

Aggressively, she removed row after row of books from the shelves, and it was not until she reached the fourth shelf that a click was heard. She did not realize it at first, but simultaneously with the removal of the books, the shelf tipped down to one side, activating the latch and springing the door ajar.

She was ecstatic, never feeling more joyful in her entire life. It was as if she had found a pot full of gold. Most ingenious, she thought. As she studied the mechanism, she could not help marvel over the simplicity of the device. While the shelf was balanced with books, it acted like a see saw. The activation was easily accomplished by pressing down on one side or by removing some books, causing it to tip up. As the shelf tipped, it pulled back a light cable that was attached to the latch, springing open the hidden door. It was quite extraordinary; a tipped shelf activation, and it did not even require a key or electricity to operate.

As Margaret opened the bookshelf door to gaze in, her attentions were drawn to a rush of cool air that breezed across her face. At that moment, she could not help but think of Edith and the haunting experiences she had endured while napping in the parlor. Her memories were vivid as she could still recall Edith's frightening disturbance of being awakened many times by mysterious drafts emanating from a corner of the room. She had just uncovered their obvious cause, believing it had to have been Isabel who created them upon her entry.

Building up the courage, she bravely entered the open space and stood on the landing, studying the interior before she proceeded. Overshadowed by darkness, she shined her light ahead and followed the beam as her eyes darted down each step of the long stairwell.

With the rainy season now in full bloom, the atmosphere of the tunnel had become damp, and the scent of mildew was so obvious, it could not go undetected. Once descending the steps, Margaret made her way into the narrow tunnel that was constructed of fieldstone walls with a brick arch ceiling. Although she had no idea of its length, she could see that it was quite extensive as she shined her light ahead and saw that the beam did not penetrate to the other side.

Slowly proceeding and watching every step, Margaret, detesting wet feet, had no other choice but to slosh through the puddles. With the accumulation of the heavy rain that saturated the ground from the lack of good drainage, it was literary impossible for her to stay dry. Besides enduring soggy feet, she also had to contend with the constant drops of moisture that fell on her head and the countless cobwebs that draped across her face.

After covering about a quarter of a mile of the waterlogged tunnel that seemed to go on eternally, she stumbled upon a stairwell that now led upward. While standing idle as she caught her breath at the foot of the steps, Margaret could have sworn that she heard a voice. For the moment, she was uncertain if she had, and to verify her suspicion, she ascended the steps midway where again the voice was heard but this time with much more clarity.

The chatter seemed unusually strange. It was not muttering or talking in the normal way when one person communicated with another; nor was it arguing or any other discussion in the sense of rambling on as one would do while talking to oneself. It was as if someone was reciting a story, a child's story at that.

As she looked up, she noticed that the hatch had been left open. Continuing with her climb, Margaret stopped at the top and cautiously peeked over, trying to remain inconspicuous. Hidden well within the phony vault, she could see a glowing light on the far side of the crypt. Not wanting to alert Isabel of her presence by using her flashlight, she tried her best to see in the darkness to whom Isabel was reading.

Unable to see very well from where she stood, Margaret decided to position herself at another location where she could better observe Isabel and the child. Slowly, she quietly crawled out of the open space, and keeping very low, she hid behind a pillar, which offered a closer view. There she could clearly see Isabel from the side, sitting slouched over in front of several candles while holding a child's storybook in her hand. She had no doubt in her mind that Isabel was reading to someone. At that moment, many unanswered questions ran rampant through her curious mind. Who was this child? Where did he or she come from? Was it possible that Isabel had kidnapped an innocent child?

Feeling the far side of the vault must be blocking the child, Margaret, in line behind the pillar, rose to her feet, and stretching her neck as she gazed over Isabel's shoulders, she scanned the entire side of the vault.

Unfortunately and despite her best efforts, no child was detected. Then it suddenly struck her, and she realized what a fool she was. It hadn't been a child after all, at least not that of the living. With love extended far beyond the grave, it was apparent that Isabel was reading to a child, her only child, Shawn.

She now understood the cause of the wax droppings and why the children's books had been spread all over the top of the vault. As Margaret watched on, observing in silence, she could not help feeling sorry for Isabel. It was obvious that she missed Shawn dearly and loved him very much as she read each sentence, changing her expressions to imitate each of the characters in the book. Isabel acted as if Shawn was still alive and standing there before her, and being content in her own little world, she radiated smiles of joy and laughter.

For the moment, Margaret was grasped by the sentiment, and she could feel her eyes swell, wanting to cry. She could not exactly say why she felt as she did, but after seeing the yearning in Isabel's eyes, it all seemed so pitiful as she watched a broken heart inwardly mourn for her child. She could see that out of this great love there was also a great loss that was so devastating, it had torn Isabel apart. Because she was unable to accept the truth of Shawn's death, her deranged behavior was the consequence of her enduring love. In life, he was all she had, all she ever loved, and as a woman, Margaret felt nothing but sympathy for her. After all, who can say what life may bring. And if she ever loved someone as deeply as Isabel did, she might herself become a victim under the same misfortunate circumstances.

Feeling compassion, Margaret could understand the emotional strain that tormented Isabel's mind with a love so eternal that her fate had been sealed, and she had been driven into the pits of madness. Then suddenly her thoughts were interrupted as the reading abruptly stopped, and silence prevailed for a still moment.

Without a flinch of a muscle or a bat of an eye, Isabel stood stiff as a board, briefly sniffing the air. In her awareness, she gazed around the room with darting eyes, once her nose caught the sweet scent of Margaret's perfume. It was the scent of honeysuckle, a scent with which she was well familiar, and at one time, she herself had worn. At that moment, it became apparent to Margaret that her presence had somehow been detected, although she did not know how.

Immediately after the discovery, a real fear swelled within her, and she held her breath, trying not to make a sound. As she watched on, terrorized by the very thought, her face became flushed as she heard a voice bellowing in the darkness.

"I know you are there somewhere, Margaret. I can smell you. Apparently, your perfume was a good choice, and it did do you justice, my dear. But unfortunately, in your case, it was a dead giveaway. So you might as well come out."

Suddenly Margaret became flustered. For an instant, she did not know exactly what to do. Above all, she did not want to appear as a spy, observing the whole affair of Isabel's lunatic behavior. Instead, she wanted Isabel to think that her arrival from the tunnel was sudden, and she had just happened to stumble on her. But she knew she was caught red handed, and it would be foolish to try to make it appear differently. Acknowledging that it was the interview she had come for in the first place, Margaret, with a change of heart, rose to her feet and stepped out of the shadows. She had no choice now but to confront Isabel face to face.

At first, stillness and dead silence stood over them as eyes met and locked on contact. From the piercing stare and stern look on Isabel's face, Margaret knew her presence was not at all welcomed. She felt as if she had walked into the lion's den, and at any given moment, Isabel would lunge at her, ripping her apart for infringing on her privacy.

For a short while, the mood subsided, and Margaret took the courage to act on her convictions by elaborating, feeling she had much to explain, "I hope you can forgive this intrusion. I never meant to be impertinent. All I was trying to do was establish the facts in your life that were shadowed in mystery by a past that was long forgotten. During my investigation, I was under the assumption that all the members of the Laughton family were deceased. Little did I know the reality of your true identity. Although I admit I was taken by storm by the sudden discovery, I also came to know the significance of the name Desa and how much it truly meant to you. Once your existence was revealed, I was driven on a course, overwhelmed by a compulsion to seek out the truth. Though your life may have been shrouded by much controversy and secrecy, what I found most fascinating was how you faked your death and deluded the town into believing that you had died by keeping your existence hidden from the public's eyes. It was by that same token of fascination that I was jolted even further by the mere fact of your age and your ability to prolong your life for one hundred twenty-five years."

Feeling slightly less apprehensive, although she knew at any moment Isabel could end her life, Margaret continued, "Through my extensive interview with Inspector Gibbs, his accuracy and depth of the events of your life excited me enormously, so much so, that I feel that I have come to know you as well as I know myself. I have learned of your suffering, your persecution, your acrimony, and even your murders, all premeditated and covered up in a fashion to look like accidents. Your life was truly incredible, an untold story of a woman who balanced the scale between life and death for the love and protection of her son.

"It was unfortunate on that awful day that the scale first tipped, as your son became a victim of harsh persecution by the town settlers, prompting a wild, uncontrollable chain of events that led to several murders," Margaret rambled on as if she were writing her article. "You were deprived of justice, betrayed by the very system you believed in, and driven on a path of murder, outraged and blinded by revenge. I can understand your bitterness as you swore a mother's scorn on all those who were involved, making certain that they paid dearly for what they had done. Yet the rampage did not stop there. In order to safeguard your son and keep from losing him, the deaths continued, thereafter, for each one who posed a threat."

Not knowing what was going on in Isabel's head as she just stood there, never saying a word, Margaret thought it best to center on Shawn. "I'm aware how much you adored Shawn and worshipped the ground he walked on. I also understand that losing him would have killed you and because you were so afraid of that one concept, you became distraught, losing all sense of reason and sensibility. I am sorry I have awakened the past and reminded you of a time that brought you nothing but hardship and pain. Even now, as I stand here before you, I tremble knowing of your extraordinary powers, which you could dispense with a mere thought. I assure you I have not come as a foe, but as a friend, extending my hand and offering my sincere sympathy to both you and your son."

With her hand extended, Margaret paused, embracing the silence of the gesture. It was soon after her expressed emotion, she continued in a low voice, this time using diplomacy to seek an answer to a puzzling question. "After everything I have learned about your life, there is still one thing that tantalizes my curiosity. I cannot understand why all those who opposed you met swift, horrible deaths, yet you spared Inspector Gibbs' life, for some unknown reason, despite his potential threat, knowing of all your murders. Even with Inspector Gibbs' remarkable memory, as he recalled every detail vividly, that was the one recollection he could not explain nor understand. What motivated your decision?"

"Although you attempt to sugar-coat my life with sweet talk, there was much wrongdoing in my life for which I am not at all proud and still haunts me today. Not that you deserve one, nevertheless, I will satisfy you with an explanation, just to please myself. You see, Inspector Gibbs was sort of like you in a way. Very much dedicated in his work and could not be persuaded to alter his principles by letting certain matters be overlooked. Out of everyone with whom I was associated, he was the only person who showed us a bit of kindness, and I could not find it in my heart to kill him after he had helped my son. But let me not bore you with the turmoil of my life. I, somehow, have the funny notion that there is something else, something more, you want to tell me, and as a journalist, I doubt very much you came here just to enlighten me on the biography of my life."

Margaret, deepened in shame and denial, realized she was not dealing with any ordinary person. Well aware of Isabel's power and physic ability to foresee things and not wishing to anger her any more than she already had, she decided to come clean, feeling she could better her chances with the truth. "Please allow me to be frank. I would like to apologize for giving you the wrong impression for my motives. I realize I may have overstepped my bounds, but ever since your identity was revealed to me, I feel I have stumbled onto one of the greatest discoveries of the decade. The phenomenon of your age and life would demonstrate to the world a remarkable achievement, living proof of a person's ability to prolong life for one hundred twenty-five years. All that would be required from you are a few photos and an interview, which would be enough for me to complete my book. I have no doubt that it would be a best seller, drawing in millions within the first publication.

"Not only that," Margaret continued, hardly taking a breath and talking extremely fast, "we could make millions more with your secret of extended life. Just think what a person would pay to live beyond the means of a normal lifespan. We would gain wealth beyond our wildest imaginations, and I would be willing to share it all with you for some of your cooperation. You don't have to rush into it. Take as much time as you need, and we can always sort out the differences with which you feel uncomfortable."

******

Right from the start, Isabel could see that Margaret was an ambitious woman. Feeling annoyed that her privacy had been invaded, she made her discontent and reluctance known under no uncertain terms. With her anger heightened, degenerating to a guttural, raspy voice, she bellowed, "How can you possibly ask this of me? After I have gone to great lengths to falsify my death, your book, in a single day, would wipe out what it took me years to accomplish. Once my existence would be brought to light, the discovery would open new avenues, prompting a reinstatement of another investigation. With Inspector Gibbs' acute memory, his accusations alone of each murder would place me in the spotlight, and the commencement of an intense witch-hunt would be underway where the law would be undeterred until I was brought to justice. I would be signing my own death warrant, and it would be as if I was admitting to all the crimes I was allegedly accused. I refuse to die in a cell, caged like some wild beast, and be a spectacle to a blood thirsty mob, drooling over the observance of my execution."

Pausing for a moment, Isabel stared into Margaret's eyes and questioned, "Do you twitch when you think of death, Margaret? Would you be afraid? When death is near, you learn to embrace it and come to terms with oneself. For you, the worldly pleasures are just beginning; you are young, full of vigor, and willing to take on all challenges. For me, the worldly pleasures have diminished; my youth has long dwindled, and there is no incentive for me to live any longer. I know the end is near; I can feel it in my bones. Whatever time is remaining, I prefer to live here, undisturbed and away from society. I have no desire for riches or comfort and am quite content despite my gloomy surroundings. I promised Shawn that I would always be by his side, and I will have it no other way. From the look on your face, I can see you have difficulty understanding my motives, but I assure you I've never been happier. You are a very brilliant woman who worked hard on this assignment, and what I am about to propose will be a lot to ask. You have everything needed from your investigation to make your book a great success. The one thing that I ask is to keep my death buried in the past. You would still have your fame and fortune, but it would have to be without my participation."

Again, Margaret's journalistic instinct got in the way of her better judgment as she was reluctant to yield to Isabel's request. With a desperate need for a solution, she took a different approach, hoping to persuade Isabel into accepting a proposition. Prompted by her inflated self-esteem, she displayed an outward show of boldness, and overstepping the bounds once again, she gave little thought to the consequences of her actions. With persistence, she once again pressured Isabel. "All right, I can understand your position with the law and your desire to remain anonymous. But there are other ways to remedy this problem without developing any drawbacks. We could still have the interview as well as photo shoots, and I will give you my solemn oath that I will keep your identity confidential. Or if you like and feel more comfortable with this suggestion, we can proceed as planned, and I will wait until your death before I submit my findings for publication. This way you will never need to be concerned about any reprisal. What do you think?"

Feeling utterly disgusted, Isabel could see that there was no point in continuing. Blinded by her eagerness and motivated by her thoughts of wealth, she could see the anxiousness for fame that filled Margaret's eyes. Apparently, she had made up her mind and would stop at nothing to achieve her goal.

Annoyed by her persistence, Isabel refused to be manipulated and wanted nothing more than to be left alone with no part of Margaret's generous offer. Mostly, she felt her private world had been invaded and Margaret had interrupted her life, which she had spent years concealing. Feeling uneasy, she had no trust or belief in any promises that Margaret made. Troubled deeply, she realized that there was no way she could negotiate with her or allow this discovery to be publicized.

Waiting for a reply while Isabel was deep in thought, Margaret felt it best to assure Isabel once again in order to ease her mind and settle any doubts she might have. In a final pitch, she emphasized, "If you are worried, don't be. I promise you as a professional I will not say a word to anyone, no matter what. You can trust me on that."

Snapping back, Isabel quickly responded, "I'm more than sure you won't say a word!" Angelic, and yet at the same time, her smile seemed tinged with hidden implications.

Finding the tone to be strangely peculiar, Margaret's intuition warned her that there was much more to the remark, as if Isabel was insinuating some sort of threat. She tried to look beyond the smile, behind its true meaning. Withered by a scornful look, she could not help feeling that there was something sinister, something quite definite, going to happen.

******

Tuesday morning Gibbs rose to a brilliant day. Like every other day, he casually walked into the solarium for breakfast and stopped momentarily to chat with a few friends. Sitting in his usual chair that faced east, the rays of the sun, peeking out over the horizon, warmed his aging body.

While he poured himself a cup of tea, he took notice of the morning newspaper, conveniently left at the table's edge for the residents' pleasure. Face down, he nonchalantly picked it up, thumbing through the pages quickly. It was then as he turned to page six that he became flabbergasted. He recognized the woman pictured in the article. With mouth gaping and eyes bulging, he stared in disbelief. The bold letters of the headline seemed to jump out at him. Stunned and trembling with fear, he read,

Amnesia Victim, Missing Finger, Mysteriously Wandering Streets of Colchester!

Printed in the United States
63298LVS00003B/301

9 781424 129423